To Kevin —
You are the real Treasure!

The Pirate's Bastard

Nominated for the Sir Walter Raleigh Award
for Fiction, 2011.

BROAD CREEK PRESS, 2012

Laura S. Wharton

LAURA S. WHARTON

The Pirate's Bastard
© 2012 by Laura S. Wharton

Address all inquires to Laura S. Wharton
Broad Creek Press
P.O. Box 43
Mount Airy, NC 27030

Library of Congress Control Number: 2012904478

Wharton, Laura S.
The Pirate's Bastard / by Laura S. Wharton.
Mt. Airy, NC: Broad Creek Press, 2011.
p. cm.
ISBN 978-0-9837148-5-9

Historical Adventure—Fiction. 2. Pirates—Fiction.
3. Shipbuilding—Fiction. 4. North Carolina—Fiction.
813'.54
Author Photo by William L.B. Wharton
Cover Design by Sonia Crouse
Interior Design by Fusion Creative Works

Second Edition

Printed in the United States of America.

For signed copies, visit www.laurawhartonbooks.com
Wholesale copies available through Ingram.

Reviews of

The Pirate's Bastard

A fine addition to any historical fiction collection.
Having a pirate for a father leads to more harm than good. "The Pirate's Bastard" is an adventurous tale following Edward Marshall as he's dragged into his father's trade by Ignatius Pell, a friend of his father and has plenty of blackmail to counter Edward's protests. A fun story of treasure hunting and the notoriety of the father, "The Pirate's Bastard" is a fine addition to any historical fiction collection.

~ Midwest Book Review

This is a very well written and entertaining book.
~ Latitudes & Attitudes Magazine

One of the best historical fictions I have read.
This mystery of the mid-1700s is told briskly and interestingly. In fact, it is one of the best historical fictions I have read about Stede Bonnet. Wharton is so descriptive with words, which adds greatly to the suspense in this love story. Written with imagery and mounting intensity, I could not put this book down.

~Jackie Iler, *State Port Pilot* Newspaper

An excellent read.

Ms. Wharton has impressed me by the amount of time she has spent making sure everything was correct for the time period that this book takes place in. Everything is right on the mark. This book is Historical Fiction and an excellent read.

~Sandra Heptinstall, Whispering Winds Book Reviews

A must read.

Author Laura Wharton brings to light what is still so prevalent today: judgment by wealth, race, class and heritage. Let's hope she brings him and his crew back for a sequel so we can find out what is next for Edward Marshall. Well written and fast paced filled with interesting stories about ship building, the colonies and plantation life, author Laura Wharton brings to life a interesting period in time and we learn that Edward Marshall is much more than just a Pirate's Bastard. I never give stars to books that I feel are outstanding and a must read; instead, I give this book Five Beautifully Crafted Ships Edward to sail around the world and find his better place.

~ Fran Lewis, New York Reviewer

All that's missing is the big screen!

Wharton's vivid attention to maritime detail transported me to the 1700s to the sugar plantations of Barbados, then to the shipyards of Brunswick, North Carolina. I was riveted to the tale of young Edward Marshall, illegitimate son of pirate, Stede Bonnet and his French mistress. In Edward's quest to be accepted into society and ultimately a life at sea, he becomes entangled in dark secrets, a tempting treasure hunt, a chance at love, and worst of all, blackmail. The Pirate's Bastard is a must-read for young and old craving a salty bit of adventure! All that's missing is the big screen!

～ Mary Flinn, author of *The One*, *Second Time's a Charm*, and *Three Gifts*

Dedication

To my parents:

Everyone should be so loved.

PROLOGUE

Chink. Chink. Chink.

Two figures stood shoulder deep in a hole. Moonlight bounced from shovel to shovel, each digging deeper and deeper into the sand in rhythm as the men patiently took turns at the task.

Shadows moving in the dark, their motion contrasted the stillness of a third man who stood apart from them like a statue, above the hole, above the commotion. A ship's lantern casting an eerie glow about his figure, its glow reflecting on brass buttons. A slight breeze ruffled cuffs of his tailored shirt and swayed the plume in his fashionable hat.

The commander of the shore party looked on quietly as his two men dug deeper and deeper into the dune under the gnarled oak tree. At his side lay a large wooden box, barely visible under the moon's glow.

"Tsk, tsk. Better 'urry it up, mate, the Captain wants to get out on the next tide," whispered one laborer to the other, hushed by the gravity of the task. His gravely voice bore a cockney accent.

"Oui, de man is half ou' of his mind, no?", came his companion's whispered response in French Caribbean dialect. "To do this now when dey is so close behind us … but it is his most valuable treasure, no? Perhaps we will come back for it later."

"Perhaps. Well, get on with it then, will ye?"

The sound of the shovels slowed to a stop and the two men jettisoned their shovels out of the hole before hoisting themselves out. They moved slowly over to the planked box and each grabbed a side, preparing to lower it into the ground, struggling a bit under its weight. Carefully positioned over the hole, they lowered the box in place and reached for their shovels again. But before they could start to fill the hole with sand, their commander grabbed one by the arm.

"Wait." His voice was steady, firm, and unemotional.

He reached under the tree and pulled a handful of deep orange and black sand daisies from a clump, and dropped them into the hole on top of the box. He looked after the box only one more time, and turned slowly away. Walking from the tree, and the hole, he soon became one more shadow in the night. He made his way to a longboat that was pulled up on the sand and waited for the two laborers to finish their task.

A large ship stood at the ready several hundred yards off shore, to take the men on to their next destination and conquest. Yet this buried treasure held one man's heart, and all aboard the ship knew that its location would never be forgotten.

Watching the man reach the longboat, the laborer in charge on the dune turned to his companion. "That will be the end of us, I tell ye. Start yer shoveling, so we can get out of this place."

"Oui, I feel 'tis bad," muttered the other man. "There is something here that makes me not want to ever return." He started shoveling quickly, filling the hole with sand.

Chink, chink, chink. Their shoveled cadence matched the waves rolling on the shore.

Chapter One

Barbados, 1726

E dward raced down a narrow dirt street, his brown knickers torn and his raggedy shirt dirty. He looked a mess for all of his nine years, but not too unlike the other boys chasing him through the streets of Bridgetown on this bright sunny day. The seven of them ran in a tight pack after him, yelling, taunting him, hurling pebbles:

> *Aye you are a bastard,*
> *your father's up and run,*
> *aye you are a bastard,*
> *what evil he has done.*

Edward winced as a sharp stone struck his shoulder, the pain urging him to sprint. He was a loner. He was an orphan, that was true, but worse than that, he was the orphaned son of a pirate and his French mistress. He was the pirate's bastard, and that in and of itself was enough for the town's people to hate him. A constant reminder of the gentleman-gone-a-pirating, Edward represented the total sum of all evils in one skinny little boy.

Your mother was a whore,
a lady of the night,
She bloomed aboard the ship
when no island was in sight.

Edward knew that his father, Stede Bonnet, had brought shame and notoriety to their peaceful island and humiliation to his lawful wife. He heard the rumors of how she was the real head of the Bonnet household, even while Stede was about on their sugar plantation.

More a man than he, she was,
a stronger one you'll not find.
Steer clear of Ol' Mrs. Bonnet,
Or her words will not be kind.

After Stede went off to sea, the most proper Mrs. Bonnet continued to run the plantation profitably, despite her withdrawal from the island's social events. It was rare to find a woman of her fine upbringing running such a large plantation, yet it was rarer still to find a woman of her generation and stature who would withstand the knowing glances of passersby on the streets or in the meeting house. Rather than pay them any heed, she stuck to business and made a good profit at it. Perhaps she felt that Bonnet would return to his senses--and return to her for a tongue-lashing he would not soon forget.

On more than one instance, Edward stole away from the school grounds before the pack of town kids and other orphans saw him, and he made his way to the Bonnet plantation just outside of Bridgetown. He crept around the property, hoping to come up with answers to questions about his father. What kind of a man would leave all this behind? He clearly had wealth, more than Edward would ever know. He had slaves, and plenty of them. What kind of a master was he?

As he made his way around the perimeter of the plantation, Edward counted six different chattel houses, each with a red roof covering white-washed stucco and timbered walls and adorned with bright green shutters that helped keep out the heat of the day. These small structures were moved to various parts of the plantation, depending on the crops being harvested.

Bonnet had a grand house—as grand as any on the island, from what Edward could see. Its bougainvillea-wrapped columns held a massive second story and portico. Floor to ceiling windows and doors were protected from rain by a large covered porch and shuttered against the heat with the same kind of slatted shudders that were on the chattel houses. Edward was struck by the immensity of the house: it was three times bigger than the orphanage.

Edward would watch Mrs. Bonnet move around the house's immediate grounds from a safe distance. She didn't look like the monster Edward felt sure she would be, given the songs the other children sang intending him to hear. Still, he did not want to get close enough to be found out by her.

A sword through the heart for jewels,
and then he burned their ships

*Hung on the gallows in Charleston
And now in tide muck he sits."*

When word of Stede Bonnet's fate on the gallows in Charleston reached Barbados, rumors persisted that the news made Mrs. Bonnet go crazy. Edward wanted to see her because he had never seen a crazy person before, and because he felt sorry for her. She was alone, too, all because of his father. But when he visited the plantation, he lost his courage to confront her. And then he would head back to the orphanage, back to a beating for arriving late.

Edward grew weary of the daily assaults he endured from the town's children and the weighty stares from the director of the rarely-visited orphanage. But more than that, he felt sadly alone, unable to grieve a family he never knew, and unable to hope for better than the strange hand life had dealt him.

His one consolation was the friend and mentor he had found in the Reverend Jonathan Eubanks, a kind minister of the Anglican Church in Bridgetown. Since he found Edward as a small, wiggling bundle on the Church's door steps, Eubanks had done what he could to protect Edward from the storms of his young life by encouraging him to look forward and upward rather than behind him. The past was over, and there was nothing to be gained by its study. The future, on the other hand, was the one thing Edward could control.

Edward turned a corner as he ran at full speed to escape the town boys, flying in through the two massive wooden doors of a small but neat Church. As he slammed the doors fast behind him, he ran smack into Eubanks, a tall, gaunt man of forty. Dressed in a long black coat with a white collar peeping out at his throat, Eubanks would never be mistaken for the dandies who paraded around Bridgetown's streets sporting the latest fashions of wigs and brightly colored coats and hats they seemed to think were their birthright.

Edward looked up and into the stern face of Eubanks. He thought for certain he was in for a lecture about the perils of running through the Church, but Eubanks' stoic face gave way to a smile as he held the boy at arm's length and surveyed him from head to toe. Aware of his unruly appearance for the first time this day, Edward looked down and hastily tried to tuck in his torn shirt. Eubanks gently released Edward's shoulder, shook his head, and returned to a small table near the vestibule where he had laid some papers just as Edward made his grand entrance.

He clasped his hands behind his back, turned away from Edward and faced the small oak table. Without looking at Edward again, he spoke over his shoulder. "So, they are after you again, are they, my son?"

"Yes Sir, Master Eubanks. I try to be friends with them, but they continue to taunt me and to call me names. They chased me all the way from the school, and even cut me off from going to the orphanage, so now I won't get any supper because I am so late." Edward drew a heavy sigh, and looked downcast at the dark mahogany stained floor.

This Church was a refuge for him in many ways. Not only did he feel safe here from the world outside, he often helped the Reverend Eubanks with preparing the Church for regular services by cleaning the worn wooden floors until they glistened and straightening the wooden plank pews after every service. Aside from the deep respect he felt for the Reverend, Edward also knew that his efforts were appreciated. In a young life filled with so much anguish, it was the Reverend Eubanks who afforded him a little peace--and often more food than what he could get at the orphanage. The Reverend had explained on many occasions that Edward needed to be in school and live with the other boys there, though Edward hated it. He felt his treatment was harsher than anyone else's, despite that he tried to do everything right.

Eubanks turned to face Edward, and knelt down so that he could look him in the eyes. "I know, son. Yes, it is hard on you, this life your father has left you to, but you are indeed his boy, like it or not. When he left you behind, he saddled you with a terrible burden. All of your days will be spent running away from the monster that he was, I fear. But you must not grow up to be like him."

"Yes, Sir, I know what he was," Edward fidgeted, but held the Reverend's eyes. This was possibly the only person he trusted. "I wish I could get far away from here. It is not fair that I should live the rest of my life around people who cared nothing for my father. They think that I am like him. I am nothing like him!" Edward shouted, visibly shaking with emotion.

"There, there, Edward. I know you are not like he was, dear boy. You need not convince me. You are a good, kind soul, and someday you will be rewarded for your patience." Eubanks placed a steadying hand on Edward's shoulder, bracing the shaking boy who fought back tears.

"You have been of immense help to me here at the Church, and for that, you will be rewarded in heaven, praise the Lord. But these are trying times for you now, I see that. Perhaps …. Perhaps I can help you to succeed in your wish to be away from this place, but it would require great sacrifice on your part," Eubanks smiled.

Edward looked up, his tear-filled eyes brimming. "Sacrifice? What do I have to do?"

"I have just learned of my new assignment. I am to oversee the flock in a settlement called New Brunswick in the colony of Carolina," Eubanks pulled the papers from the table and showed them to Edward. He put his arm around the boy and led him up the center aisle that separated the men from the women during services. "Come with me, and we shall discuss it further."

Edward glanced at the ceiling—a design he had come to memorize by heart over the years he attended services and helped the Reverend. Built with timbered beams like the inside of a ship, the ceiling was plain except for the three small tiered candleholders suspended from the center beams which were lowered to be lit and raised back in place by a pulley system.

The two made their way through a door to the left of the pulpit, and entered a small room where the Reverend wrote his sermons, prepared his meals over a small fireplace, and greeted members of his congregation from time to time. This room was the public room for his accommodations provided by the Church, and though it was small, Eubanks often remarked that it was adequate for a man of the cloth. There were also two smaller anterooms that had been added on in rabbit-warren fashion before his arrival in Barbados. One held his rope-cradled mattress, a freestanding pine wardrobe that contained a second long black coat and white shirt, and a washbasin and pitcher. The second room, even smaller than the first, held food stores and donations from his congregation. These made up the contents of his pantry, and more often than not, Eubanks gave most of his meager provisions to those whom he deemed in need.

Eubanks continued. "This colony is developing quite well, and those who have visited the land say that life there is rich with promise. As you are my ward, you could come with me to this new place and help me establish roots for the Anglican Church. If you come with me, it shall be required of you to work with me for a time of seven years. Upon completion of your service, you would be free to explore the New World on your own. If you would prefer not to leave this island now, you may stay behind and become the ward of the Crown. I would not be able to protect you from this life that you have come to dread, but at least you would be in familiar surroundings. I am giving you this choice to make, because life in the new colony will not always be easy. You will go without a name, without a heritage, which can be a challenge as well as a blessing, and what you earn from your own hard work will be your only inheritance. What do you fancy?"

"A new life in the New World!" Edward shouted and jumped for joy. "To be where no one knows who I am or where I came from ... that is my wish. Please take me with you, and I shall prove a worthy servant to you and to the Church! Tell me more!" Edward grabbed the Reverend's hand and led him to a chair, plopping himself on the floor beside the chair.

"My word! You are excitable, are you not?" Eubanks steadied himself in the chair, which arched back a bit when Edward heartily pushed him into it. "Well, this new township was founded earlier this year by Mister Maurice Moore, the son of James Moore, Governor of South Carolina. It is a port town, and it is said that there is a wealth of longleaf pine trees from whence come naval stores good for building ships. The people there are from other colonies, as well as from our own island, and indeed other countries, including Scotland and England—gone to seek their fortunes, no doubt--but they need the judicious hand of the Lord to guide them in their endeavors. It has been put to me to undertake the task of ministering to their souls. Mister Moore is a distant cousin of my mother's, and he has requested that I join him there. After some deliberation, the Church granted his request." Eubanks waved the papers he'd brought from the vestibule overhead in confirmation of the assignment.

"Beggin' your pardon, Sir, but what would you require of me?" Edward sat forward on his knees and placed his hands neatly in his lap. His dark red hair, a mess from his run, crept down in his face over his steely blue eyes. Eubanks leaned a little closer, and pushed the loose strands of hair back. Edward smiled at the attention.

"As my ward, you are to do as I say in preparing whatever structure we are offered for services, and tending to the flock as I direct. You shall be in charge of cooking my meals, and following my instruction in the way of maintaining my household. You shall not fall behind in your studies, either. For one day, you will need all that learning to help you in some endeavor."

"After a time, when my appointment to the town is to be turned over to a new minister, you shall be free to make a choice of staying on with me or leaving to seek your own way in life. Whatever wages you save during your time with me will be your own. It will be small, but it will be adequate to start a new venture elsewhere, if that is what you choose to do. Is that clear?"

"Yes, Sir, it is very clear. I shall do the best I can do to help you in every way you direct me. Thank you for such a start at a new life." Edward looked up at Eubanks with such sincerity that the Reverend felt the right decision had been made.

Standing up from the chair, Eubanks smiled broadly at Edward. "You are welcome, my boy. Now go back to the orphanage and prepare your things as we are to leave within a few days. I will speak with the director tomorrow morning. If you run into your chums, you best not tell them what you are up to, for they may make your last days that much more unbearable."

"Yes Sir, I will be ready!" Thank you!" Edward called as he raced out of the room and into the small chapel area.

Eubanks smiled and raised his hand to wave goodbye, but the boy was already several steps out of the door of the Church. The Reverend ambled to the front door to close it again, looking in the direction of the waterfront in time to catch a glimpse of Edward as he ran down the street. Smiling, he looked at a tall ship docked at the end of the pier where men of all nationalities were loading cargo and preparing her for sail. He then stepped back into the darkness of the Church, and closed the heavy wooden door.

Eubanks was not in the habit of taking boys under his wing, and this venture was quite more than he had bargained for when nine years earlier he found the infant on the steps of the Church. He felt that Edward was his responsibility somehow, and for the past few years, he tried diligently to protect the boy from hardships he knew would eventually rear up. He saw to it that Edward was comfortable in the small orphanage on the island, but enjoyed his company whenever Edward came by to volunteer his time to the Church.

Eubanks had been sent to Barbados to relieve the aging Reverend Feathersfield of his duties. Feathersfield, it was rumored, had dealings with Bonnet from time to time, and the Church was calling him back to England. Later, when it was discovered that one of the last acts Feathersfield had performed was to marry the already married pirate to his dead mistress (while Bonnet's own wife was running the family plantation only a few miles away), the Church recanted Feathersfield's ordination, and he was cast out of the Church. The last thing that Eubanks ever heard of Feathersfield was that he had traveled to Ireland.

Eubanks had embraced his new Caribbean assignment, seeing it as a way to escape the dreary climate of London. But the Caribbean heat proved to be a challenge in its own way. He looked forward to a change of seasons in the colonies, and a chance to become acquainted with the people there. They were of strong character, he assumed, and it would be good for young Edward to meet these people who were independent and self-sufficient. It seemed to Eubanks that an orphan such as Edward could have no better mentors. And if the boy were diligent in his studies, then perhaps the pirate's blood that coursed through his veins could be tamed before he grew old enough to be tempted by the dark path his father had chosen.

"May the path of righteousness be your guide, Edward, and may the Lord keep you safe from the sins of your father," Eubanks prayed aloud as he made his way back through the Church to his quarters.

Chapter Two

White canvas sails filled with trade winds moved the Prudence earnestly along the waves. Seamen putting their backs into unfurling topsails shouted at each other until lines were taunt and the last of the sails' bellies was full. Men dangled in the rigging for their tasks of securing lines, while on deck a complement of hands coiled lines and tidied the deck.

Each day of the voyage when weather permitted, Edward made his way forward to the bow and scanned the ocean. Then he would walk aft and explore sections of the decks, keeping an eye out for the crewmen moving hurriedly from one task to the next to prepare for the hoisting or furling of a sail depending on the captain's orders. Standing on the open deck amidships between two of the six cannon, Edward watched the men work aloft.

Edward was fascinated by the three-masted ship's design. The immense rigging was fastened to the decks by spider-web-like guide ropes that were thicker than the lines the crewmen used to hoist sails. They held the masts upright and were attached to the masts below each of the masts' booms. The two forward masts carried three booms each, while the one positioned farthest aft carried only two booms. This third mast, the smallest of the three, was called the mizzen. Along with its sails, it played a big part in steering the ship, assisting an unseen rudder below the waterline. The forward two masts, on the other hand, helped to add speed to the journey, harnessing the wind's energy. Each of the masts had a crow's nest platform high up, and from this vantage point, approaching ships could be identified and the dangerous coral heads blooming up through the islands' crystal waters could be spotted in time and avoided by the helmsman.

Several times during the voyage, Edward climbed into a longboat that was nestled inside a second slightly larger one. Seated comfortably on a smoothly varnished plank, he sketched the longboat's fine sweeping lines on paper with charcoal that the Reverend Eubanks provided before they departed Barbados. These tenders that he drew were used to ferry passengers and provisions to and from the ship. They also provided platforms for crewmen to tend to the ship's sides and hull below the waterline when it was in need of repairs. Just behind the longboats amidships was a cache of spare masts and yards, necessary for the long voyages out of sight of land for many days. The crewmen needed to be able to repair anything that broke, and so the ship carried its own chandlery wherever it went.

Further aft was a raised platform from which the captain and the helmsman steered the ship. When he could do it without getting fussed at by the crew, Edward would sketch the two crewmen who stood at the ready to alter the ship's course based on the captain's directions, each one taking a turn at the large wooden tiller that controlled the rudder below the waterline. The men showed Edward a compass that helped in charting the course.

"But mind you, laddie, that most experienced sea captains rely on the stars to navigate," said the lanky man in the well-worn but clean yellow shirt. Our present course," he explained, "is an easy passage, and it's possible to stay within sight of land for most of the trip, assuming the captain wants to sail between Caribbean Islands and then up the coast and keep an eye open for familiar landmarks."

The other man chimed in. "But there's danger sailing too close to land. In addition to shoals and rocks that guard the coastline, there are still a few privateers around who keep a keen eye open for unsuspecting ships," he said, as he pointed beyond the horizon. "In general, it's better for us to stay off shore as long as possible in case of storms and unwelcome guests. Out there, there's more room to maneuver as large a ship as the *Prudence.*"

Edward was intrigued to hear about privateers--modern day pirates, he thought--who could sail the waters in search of enemy ships with the blessing of their king. This was unlike a pirate, who challenged ships regardless of nationality if there could be something to gain by a battle.

The *Prudence* was different from many of the schooners of her day. She was outfitted with six cannon that shot four pounds of lead, three on each side of the main deck of the ship, and among her crew were fighting men who knew how to use them. There were also two smaller swivel guns mounted on each side of the navigation deck that could each fire a three-fourths to one-pound shot. Many other ships of similar design had a gun deck below the main deck, but this schooner used much of that deck for cargo and livestock to afford passengers a more pleasant voyage with more room in their accommodations and less proximity to unpleasant cargo odors.

Edward shared quarters with the Reverend Eubanks on the deck below. His room had opening portals just above the waterline, and was simply appointed with two rope beds suspended by the cabin's ceiling and bolted to the sides of the room; a washstand and chamber pot; and a chair and desk over which a small lantern hung. There was additional room for sea trunks carrying personal belongings. What little clothing Edward had was tucked into a small section of one of Eubank's three bags. In general, two people were assigned to each room, or families traveling with children would take over a slightly larger room that could handle extra sleeping hammocks for children.

The captain's quarters were aft of the ship just below the helmsman's station, and once Edward peeked into the crew's quarters one deck below on the cargo deck near the livestock and spar lines. On this deck was also the galley where simple meals were prepared.

Edward and the other passengers ate meals on deck in fair weather, and it was like a grand picnic with parents and children lounging and visiting. A crew member who was handy with a fiddle could usually entice a few to dance after the evening meals for a bit of entertainment. When the weather was unkind, everyone dined down below in an area that held only long plank tables and benches.

In the belly of the ship were spare anchors and ballast, a mixture of stones, glass bricks and iron scraps. It helped to balance the ship when cargo was light. When the cargo holds were filled to capacity, ballast was then tossed overboard or left behind at the loading docks where it soon found its way into newly laid streets as paving material, or into the foundations of homes, like the ones in Brunswick, Edward would soon learn.

Edward absorbed his new surroundings like a sponge. This ship was a new world in and of itself, and he combed every inch of it as he was allowed to with paper and charcoal in hand. As he had never had the luxury of free time or such fine art tools as the ones the Reverend secured for him, Edward was only just seeing that he had talent and interest in drawing.

There were not many other children his age on board, just four children considerably younger than he who clung to their mothers' long skirts. From time to time, he sat with these small children, looking after them much to the relief of their mothers who took advantage of the moment to steal away for fresh air on deck or a sliver of private time in their cabins.

Sometimes, he took the older of the children with him on his tour of the ship.

"It is not!" One of the children yelled.

"It is so, isn't it, Edward?" The other looked earnestly at Edward as the three of them stood at the ship's rail, looking out at what appeared to be another ship on the horizon.

"I don't know if that's a pirate ship, Thomas," Edward said, smiling at the two boys. Edward had been quick to board first with the Reverend Eubanks, and thus far had evaded all questions of adult passengers, most of who were from other islands and from England. Edward was quite pleased to think that nobody on board, except the Reverend, knew of his past. Like him, all the passengers aboard were heading for the newness of the colonies. He grew more confident in his sea legs daily, and promised himself that some day he would return to the sea, not as his father had done, but for the sheer pleasure of being aboard a sailing vessel.

"It is so," the smaller boy cried, and he ran back to the spot where his mother and sisters were sitting, resting in the shade of a canopy on deck.

After several weeks of sailing, *Prudence* began the slow and arduous path toward the entrance to the Cape

Fear River. Studded with shoals of up to 30 miles, this region had a reputation for wrecking ships.

On a bright, crisp morning as Edward made his rounds on deck, he noticed crewmen scurrying more than usual. He made his way to the bow, and saw what all the commotion was about. The ship was making way into a sheltered stretch of water, the mouth of the Cape Fear River. To starboard was Smith Island, a twenty-four-acre island that varied in topography from its large oceanside dunes to its riverside maritime forest of live oak trees. To port was a low island punctuated by two inlets to smaller rivers and surrounded by grassy marshes the color of emeralds and gold in the morning sun. Edward was certain he had never seen anything more beautiful than those marshes. Unlike the white, flat beaches of his native Barbados, these islands had thin spits of sand and a skin of marsh grass protecting them from encroaching waves. Edward decided then and there that he would call himself "Marshall" after those grasses.

Ahead of the ship was what looked to be another flat island; but Edward noted the crewmen were furling the sails and making fast the lines, much the way he'd seen other ships' crews do as they secured ships in Bridgetown's harbor. He was here! He was in the New World!

Edward leaned out as far as he could over the rail. He felt a strong hand pulling him back and looked up to see the Reverend Eubanks sternly shake his head.

"What a pity it would be to come all this way and then have you fall overboard." With one hand remaining on Edward's shirt, Eubanks surveyed the land that lay in front of the ship.

Over the next two hours, the ship snaked its way from the river's entrance to its final destination, a protected area of the river directly in front of the town of Brunswick. Sails were secured and a massive anchor dropped before the longboats were manned and filled to capacity with passengers and cargo.

Edward and the Reverend were in the second longboat to make its way from the schooner toward shore. Their companions included two of the smaller children and their parents. The rest of the boat was filled with packages, provisions, and trunks. As crewmen rowed the longboats the short distance to shore, Edward took it all in, his head spinning from the sights and sounds of the river and forested shore. He could see smart-looking buildings lining the waterfront area, with warehouses at one end, and at the other end of the row he could make out what looked like two-story homes similar to what he left behind in Barbados.

"Look, Brunswick! It is just as you said it would be. There are trees here I have never seen and birds--what do you call those?" Edward pointed to a flock of white birds roosting in treetops like white small white candles on a Christmas tree.

"Those are ibis, I believe. I read an account of them in a book about wildlife in the colonies. They migrate to southern climates in winter and come back to this same place to roost and build nests for their young hatchlings.

Remember Edward, the weather here is quite different from Barbados. I understand there can be some harsh times in winter. But we will grow accustomed to the weather and the wild creatures who call this place home," he said just as the ibis flew from the trees alarmed at the longboats' intrusion.

"Do you think there are Indians here?" Edward looked thoughtfully at the Reverend and lowered his voice so as not to be overheard by the smaller children seated just ahead.

"Yes, son, I know that there are. They have been here longer than white men, but you need not fear them. They have accepted colonists into their midst because of the possibility of trade. Colonists from Virginia to the north and to the south are making this township an active port. See that tall tree over there?" Eubanks pointed out a tall, spindly pine.

Edward nodded.

"That is a long leaf pine. The colonies are filled with them. Men harvest resin--some call it sticky gold--and produce tar, pitch, and turpentine, all of which are important for building and maintaining the Royal Navy and other trade ships sailing between the colonies, the islands, and England," Eubanks explained. "Because Brunswick is located on this protected river, it will soon be one of the largest shipping ports for the exportation of these goods. You would be wise to pay attention to the manner of ships entering and leaving this port for the duration of your stay. It is my belief that your fate lies in building ships here in the New World. What say you to that?"

"If you would think that would be the path to follow, then that is where I will place my efforts," replied Edward.

Eubanks smiled at the boy, and patted him on the back gently. "You are wise beyond your years, my lad. There are, of course, many other options for you to make a livelihood here, but I noticed you seemed quite fascinated aboard the ship, so I figure you might be interested in shipbuilding as a vocation."

Edward nodded, "I did enjoy exploring the ship. That's the first time I've ever been aboard one larger than the skiff I used to go fishing in Bridgetown."

The two faced forward and watched as the town docks came into view. "What are they doing there?" Edward pointed out three men who where throwing stones into structures along the water's edge.

"Building more docks," called the oarsman seated just behind them. "Them boxes are built out of pine on shore," the man pointed to a crib-like structure waiting to be put in the water, "and then floated at the water's edge and held in place with ropes. Then stones are thrown into the boxes--that's what those men are doing now. When they get full, the boxes sink, and a layer of whole logs topped with planks makes a dock. I seen them built this way up and down the coast," the man explained. "Until these new docks are complete, we all have to use the working docks in front of the warehouse. When the tide is high," he continued, "these docks are within easy reach of most tenders; but as the tide starts to flow out as it was now, we have to climb a rope ladder to reach the docks. You'll see what I mean," he explained, as he and the forward crewman reached out and tethered the long-boat fore and aft to the raised dock's pilings, bringing it alongside. The forward crewman pulled down from the dock overhead a short rope ladder with wooden slat steps into the longboat, and held it tight for the first passenger to disembark.

For the children, the challenge of climbing the rope and slat ladder was one more game to play. They scampered up the ladder, one after the other, followed closely by Edward. Next, the parents of the children made their way none too steadily up the ladder.

Finally, Eubanks disembarked. He barely reached the top rung when he saw Edward falter and stumble like a newborn colt unsure of his gait. Laughing, he caught himself from making the same mistake by only a few inches at the top of the bluff, his laughter fading into an embarrassed cough. He could remember only one other time that he'd felt this way, and that was after the long voyage between England and Barbados.

Around passengers, the crewmen were hurriedly off-loading their cargo with the help of a block and tackle: spices, clothing and other dry goods, gun powder, furniture and trunks. Then they hastily made their way back down the bluff into the longboat for another round from shore to ship and back.

"Ah, there is my cousin, Sir Maurice Moore." Eubanks saluted a man approaching the new arrivals. The tall man wearing fine clothing walked briskly down the sandy path.

"Quickly, now, Edward. Move swiftly." He placed his hand firmly in the middle of Edward's back and pushed him toward their belongings. He pointed to the bags. Smoothing out his coat and placing a battered hat on his balding head, Eubanks gingerly stepped forward to meet the approaching men with Edward dutifully following closely behind.

"Dear Cousin!" Eubanks' voice carried over the din of activity at the water's edge. He and his cousin raised their hands in unison, and embraced for the first time in years.

"Jonathan! I am delighted to see you've made it here in one piece. I trust your voyage was uneventful?" Moore withdrew from their embrace and pumped Eubanks' hand vigorously.

Edward noticed the similarity of their faces. Both had long noses, deep-set brown eyes and oblong balding heads, the remainder of hair for both men being silver, though Mister Moore stood two inches taller than the Reverend.

"It is so good to see you again. How long has it been?" Moore smiled, still shaking hands furiously.

"Too long, Cousin. But we are here, at last. May I present to you my charge, Edward? He will be assisting me with my duties in tending to the flock here at

Brunswick." Eubanks made a sweeping gesture to include Edward in the conversation.

Edward bowed his best gentlemanly bow, and smiled broadly at Mister Moore as he placed the bags he was carrying on the ground just off the sandy path. "So pleased to make your acquaintance, Sir."

"Your charge?" Moore questioned Eubanks, and then turned smartly to Edward. "Well, lad, welcome to the New World. I am quite sure that you will find plenty here to keep you busy, whether you are tending to a flock or not." Moore grabbed Edward's hand in his and shook it long and hard. Edward winced slightly from Moore's grip, but quickly decided that this was how all the men of the New World must shake hands.

"Now, Jonathan, about your Church," Moore said as he turned to face Eubanks and started to head up the path as quickly as he'd come down it.

"Yes, I am quite anxious to see what you have in store for me, Maurice," Eubanks fell in step with Moore, and Edward scrambled to gather their bags.

"We have yet to complete the chapel, but you will be able to hold meetings in one of the homes until it is complete," Moore continued. "My brother, 'King Roger' as they call him here in these parts, bought the family property from me, so he will be close at hand to help build a chapel for you. I don't remember if you have ever met him, he is a few years younger than us. Anyway, we will meet with him later. But I suspect that you and your young charge are quite tired from your long journey. I have taken the liberty of securing you a small cottage. It is not much of a house, but it is tidy and I think you shall find it adequate quarters." The three walked up a slight incline on the lane from the river front. Moore pointed out carpenters who were assisting homeowners build their homes set on stone foundations and mentioned some of the other buildings that were yet to come along their path.

Edward followed behind the men with the satchels, looking first to the right, then to the left, taking in the town. The three made their way toward a small lane where homes in various stages of completion stood. At the very end of the lane in front of them was a small house which would be Eubanks' home. Next to it was a garden plot where two men dressed in buckskin britches worked. A woman in a long flowing skirt and full bonnet leaned over a basket filled with vegetables she had just picked from the garden. She stood upright and curtsied to Moore as he and the newcomers passed by.

"We have no need for fancy accommodations, Maurice." Eubanks smiled at the luxury of living in a small cabin rather than the back room of his former Church. "I am sure that whatever you have selected for us will be sufficient. Praise the Lord that you have been blessed in the founding of this township. It looks very promising. My young friend here has a keen interest in ships. Perchance you could take us around on the morrow to the docks so that he might make himself known to those who build ships?"

Edward looked at the Reverend in amazement, excited about the chance to actually see shipbuilders at work.

"Indeed I shall," exclaimed Moore. "It is good to have an eye toward a trade, young man. I will introduce you to some other young men," Moore spoke over his shoulder at Edward. "Right this way. Edward, is it?" Moore motioned ahead of the trio toward the front door.

Edward nodded again, struggling to keep up with his long-legged companions. "Yes, Sir. I would be honored to see how ships are built, if that suits the Reverend's morning," he said hopefully.

Eubanks feigned exasperation, then broke out into a smile. "Certainly, son, you are free to go with Master Moore in the morning after you set to your chores and your studies. But I will be in need of your assistance to prepare the evening meal. We shall discuss it later this evening. Right now, I say I am ready for a bit of rest.

Edward nodded quickly, happily, "Yes, Sir!"

CHAPTER THREE

1791

"Watch out, planks coming through!" Edward called the familiar refrain as he hoisted a stack of planks four deep and two feet wide up on his broad shoulder before making his way beside the half-skeleton of the hull under construction in the boatyard. Two men moved out of his path to the underpinnings of the hull's cradle, then resumed their hammering of nails into the massive oak beams that would eventually form the ship's spine. Every so often, another worker would pass, using the same refrain to alert everyone of the load--and the progress of construction.

"Today's been a good day," Edward thought, as he looked up at the growing vessel. With the full boat-yard crew working on her, this boat would be done ahead of schedule after a year's work--and that meant there could be a bonus from her owner.

When he started as a boatyard apprentice all those years ago, Edward's duties increased daily from cleaning up wood shavings and gathering necessary supplies to assisting on the building of small dories that would ferry supplies to and from larger ships whose deep drafts prohibited them from approaching the wharves because of thin waters.

By the age of twelve, Edward had built his first six-foot dory by himself. Within the next year, he took creative liberties with the design of that small boat, and created a skiff with a slightly curved hull resembling an hourglass, a design that proved to increase rowing speeds over its flat-bottomed skiff predecessor. By age sixteen, when his service to the Reverend Eubanks officially ended, Edward graduated to a level of boat building apprenticeship that entitled him to work on larger crafts, and he began working directly under Matty Trumbell, owner of the growing boatyard in Brunswick. Now at age twenty-four, Edward, his best friend Richard Compton, and twelve other men from the town and the surrounding countryside built the ships for which the town was becoming well known.

Their smaller forty-foot sloops were their favorite design to work on, but it was the larger, eighty-foot pilot schooners that grew to be well respected as coastal transport ships after a few years. The ship they were currently working on was a schooner that was being built for a Mister William Leslie of Virginia who wanted a ship for trading with colonies to the south. Her christening was anticipated for December, a mere six months away.

The Brunswick designs were comparable to those from the northern colonies with one exception: their drafts were shallower to handle the shoals of the region. Between Brunswick and the fledgling town of Wilmington to the north, for instance, the Cape Fear River ran over shoals and shallow water through which deeper keeled ships could not travel without a well-trained helmsman, or pilot, as they were called. The Brunswick boats could be used by just about anyone in the narrow channel and just outside it without fear of grounding. In fact, merchants, craftsmen, and farmers sought these boats out to carry their wares up and down the coast to different ports. Smaller than their northern frigate cousins, the coastal schooners were still referred to as "hen frigates" because they carried wives and children aboard to be with their merchant husbands. And though they usually never ventured too far off shore, Brunswick ships were known to travel far to the south, and some even on to the Caribbean spice route for trade with island nations.

Edward's friend Richard knew the sailors' stories all too well. Having grown up the son of a sailor on one of these hen frigates, Richard traveled with his parents and brothers to southern ports. And for every port he visited as a child, his vivid memories made for great stories at the end of the workday.

Matty, with sailing in his veins, was the son of a coastal merchant in Massachusetts. As a younger man, Matty had sailed on ships large and small, but as his failing health became a hindrance on board, he turned to building the ships he so loved to sail. Several years earlier, he'd sailed into these waters, and claimed to have fallen in love with a young lass on the rough-hewn docks that pierced the river's edge. It was here that they met, and it was here that they married. Four years later, he had two daughters of his own to watch out for. He told Edward and Richard his sea stories most every evening when they were finishing up for the day, and at the end of each one, there was a "lesson he learnt" about the ways of others. In addition to enjoying spinning a good yarn, he wanted to teach his counterparts these lessons so they would not have to learn them the hard way as he had.

Edward longed to have stories of his own to share. He had been to sea to test some of the elements of his small-boat designs, but never had he sailed to distant ports in the islands since his arrival in town.

Brunswick was his home, and yet there was an indescribable yearning to return to the place of his birth. Edward was ready to see first hand, through the eyes of an adult, where he came from. At the same time, the thought of doing so repulsed him, for it would mean that he actually identified himself as the son of a man he detested. He put the longings out of his mind, and returned his thoughts to his work. His goals for a future did <u>not</u> include any reclaiming of the Bonnet name or rights. It was his past, he reminded himself. It was not his future.

His future, he knew, was in shipbuilding. And his future depended on funding so that he could own a merchant ship, on which he could carry great stores of goods, and a ship of which he would not be ashamed to call his home. Everyday, he tried to do something toward this goal. He had even started building his own scaled-down pilot schooner in a small shed behind his house when he was not laboring on someone else's ship.

When he finished a day's work, Edward would take his wages and put them a safe place in a crack on an interior wall of his small cottage's foundation that was built from ballast stones. He figured that it would be safe tucked away there for the time it would take him to complete his ship.

Even though he had completed his agreed-upon service with the Reverend Eubanks and had purchased his own cottage several years earlier, he still helped Eubanks, who was getting on in years. The company they kept meant much to Edward, as he considered Eubanks his father.

Edward also worked for Roger "King" Moore who was building a grand home on a neighboring tract overlooking the Brunswick River, a narrow spit of brackish water that meandered away from the Cape Fear River. Moore's rice plantation was doing very well, and he talked of trade in other colonies. He considered raising silk worms for silk production, but the region's climate was sometimes unpredictable and not entirely favorable for the worms' preferred habitat, Italian mulberry trees. Neighboring plantations had tried this as far north as Pender Precinct with limited success.

Orton was the first of many plantations in the area to grow rice, and its superior rice land of 225 acres produced well over 10,000 bushels of rice to be exported to the northern colonies, England, and other countries. In addition to his rice fields, Moore was experimenting with indigo, which could be used as a dye for cloth. The women of Brunswick delighted in the subtle shade of blue, and Moore was sure other women would enjoy it as well. His nearest competition was to the south in Georgetown and Charleston where plantations that lined the water's edge grew rice as well as indigo just as Moore did.

Cut into squares like a patchwork quilt, Orton Plantation's fields were sectioned by dikes. This exactly-cut pattern of fields and dikes was fed water by main man-made canals filled with tidal waters. Sluice gates at the head of each canal controlled the water's flow into the fields, and could be raised or lowered to maintain the proper amount of water needed at each stage of rice cultivation. Each ditch also had a much smaller gate that controlled the level of water in each field. This complicated system of gates allowed Moore's foremen to flood fields according to the rise and fall of the River's tides. After each field was flooded to the desired level, gates were closed to maintain that level.

In the evenings, Edward rowed his small dory past the entire line of river "gates" that flooded the rice fields with each tide. If any needed mending, it was his job to tend to it. And for his efforts, Edward gained a little more in wages every week. This he added to his stash in his cottage's foundation of ballast.

Rarely did he spend his growing fortune on things he did not need. He felt that if he worked hard, and eventually sold his cottage to one of the many new colonists who came to the area, he would be prepared financially to finish the ship that would carry him on his way.

Knowing of Edward's eagerness to become the master of his own ship, King Moore devised a plan that would benefit them both. In the process of clearing land for his plantation, he had amassed quite a bit of timber that was dry, milled and ready for use in shipbuilding, home-building, or some other purpose. The region was well known for its timber and sap, and Moore saw these as viable crops to add to the others of his plantation. Seeing Edward's desire to work hard, Moore had a proposition in mind.

"And how were the gates this evening, Edward?" he asked, as he counted out Edward's weekly wages on the wooden platform that served as a landing where he met Edward weekly.

"They are all in good repair," Edward reported. He took his money and shoved it deeply into the palm of a gloved hand. His relationship with King had developed into something comfortable for Edward. He viewed King as an uncle figure, someone whom he respected and trusted. Like the Reverend, King had qualities that Edward admired and wanted to emulate. He saw King's success, and sought the same for himself--but on his own terms. This arrangement of mending gates was a way that Edward could get what he wanted financially, and learn more about what it takes to run a plantation the magni-tude of this size in the event that he decided later in life to do so.

"Edward, how would you like to earn a bit more for your troubles?" posed King.

"You know I am interested. What have you in mind?"

"I have a goodly amount of timber that I should like to sell through a broker in Wilmington just up the road, and I certainly do not have the time to take a sample to him. Would you be interested in being my personal representative for a fee?"

"That would suit me fine, Edward beamed. "When would you like me to leave?" Eager to impress King, Edward jumped at the opportunity.

Gesturing to a three-foot high stack of freshly cut timber and an adjacent stack of milled lumber, King suggested, "I am thinking that if you and your man load up one of my wagons with some samples of this wood in a day or two, you could make the trip before next week. I will pay you a handsome percentage for whatever you are able to sell. You will want to look up a Mister Thaddeus Jenkins. He deals with buyers who want good lumber for shipbuilding and for home building, and he is a fair man. You will find him at the new warehouse on the wharf, the one that is on the waterfront."

Edward paused before speaking. "Is this wood something that could be helpful in building our local ships?"

With a broad smile, King patted Edward on the shoulder. He was pleased that Edward would think of his own projects first, but knew that the local shipyard was in no position to pay him what he wanted for the goods. Besides, there was plenty of this renewable resource to go around, and the Brunswick yard where Edward worked could only produce a few small boats in a year, so there was time for more trees to mature for future projects.

"It seems that we have enough in our own area for the local shipyard's use, so we might as well make a little extra on what we can offer to Jenkins. You will know him by his, um, shall we say, stout presence, Edward. He usually can be found in the thicket of commerce, so you may ask for him by name when you get to Wilmington."

Edward thanked King, both for his weekly wages and for the opportunity to earn more. As he made his way home, he marveled at how King worked and seemingly expanded his ventures daily.

But Edward was learning another lesson here, one that slowly came to light after many evenings' work: by watching King deal with his foremen and his slaves around the plantation grounds, Edward began to realize the kinds of demands that surely his own father had been under back on his sugar plantation in Barbados. Such demands obviously made men like King stronger. Edward wondered about Stede's strength and character before he chose to go a-pirating: what kind of a man was he? What was his home life like? Was he a fair master of his slaves? Edward wondered if his father was involved in the day-to-day operations of his plantation, or if he left its running in the capable hands of a foreman. All of these questions he pondered each night as he rowed from gate to gate. And with each pull of his oars, he wondered of he would ever learn more of that side to his father's life.

Once home, Edward raised the wick in his oil lamp and lit it. Soon, his cottage was aglow in a wash of pale light. He carefully placed his wages in among the safety of the cottage's foundation, and rummaged around for something to eat. After washing up, he lowered the wick in the lamp, and retired for the evening. His thoughts were slow to retire, though, as Edward tossed and turned. A trip to Wilmington was not something to be taken lightly. He mulled over how he would approach this person Jenkins, and began to look forward to it. In the morning, he would consult the Reverend, and find Elijah.

Somewhere in his late forties, Elijah had told Edward that he was a free man who as a slave had served his time on a plantation in Charleston, and had gradually bought his freedom. His hard work, both for his master and for a local shipyard that "rented" his services for a fee earned Elijah recognition as a diligent worker who could be trusted with nearly any task. And for his efforts (and for a price), he was soon set free. Finding Charleston a closed society for free men of color where he'd have to show a pass and papers nearly everyday or be considered a runaway slave, Elijah headed north and eventually made his way to Brunswick when it was first being built.

Elijah and Edward met several years later when Matty hired him to help build ships. Edward soon joined the shipyard as a young apprentice, and Elijah took it upon himself to mentor him.

As years passed, and Elijah and Edward grew fond of each other, often tackling boatyard tasks together. Their time together grew daily, and before long, Edward considered Elijah to be a trustworthy and true friend, ignoring the color of his skin. Many people, like Moore, thought that Elijah was Edward's slave, as they spent so much time together; but Elijah told Edward time and again that other peoples' opinions meant little to him--as long as Edward had his own about their friendship. And Edward never turned his back on his friend.

The following day, Saturday, Edward headed directly past the shipyard up the hill to the church where he knew he would find Eubanks. As was his custom, Eubanks often started the day with early morning prayers there, and he often expressed to his congregation that he would welcome other people during that time. Eubanks also used this time to visit the sick, or tend to related church matters such as updating records. On this particular day, Eubanks was noting that were two births--twins--to the Andersens. Both healthy girls, they would soon find their way to the baptizing bowl as he called a small tidal pool at the river's edge.

"Reverend, good morning," called Edward, as he entered the church. Eubanks stood up from his work, his back starting to curve under the weight of his years. Upon seeing Edward, his face lit up and he strode a few feet to meet Edward and usher him to his table.

"So good to see you, Edward, you seldom come to visit aside from the Sabbath, I was beginning to think you had forgotten your old friend." Eubanks motioned Edward to sit. Their relationship was long and strong, and Edward still relied on his sound advice. Eubanks never failed in sharing his wisdom, and today was no exception. Upon hearing of Edward's plans to visit Wilmington, Eubanks conveyed his satisfaction at the young man's good business sense.

"Cousin is always up to something, it seems," he smiled. "But this is a good thing he has offered you, and I am pleased to hear that you trust him enough to take him up on his offer. I would advise you to keep your wits about you in dealing with anyone who sells for a living, son. They sometimes have a way of selling what is not needed." Eubanks let a sly smile creep across his face. "But, come to think of it, in this case, you are the salesman, are you not?"

Edward nodded.

"Well, that being the case, keep your own counsel. As I have said in the past, be careful not to volunteer too much information, especially when asked questions. Answer them honestly, to be sure, but do not divulge more than the question calls for--this is good advice for all of your dealings, but no more so than when dealing with strangers where money is concerned."

"That sounds like good advice, Reverend. I will keep what I know tucked in my hat. I do trust that Moore knows the fellow to whom he wishes to sell his lumber."

"You are taking Elijah? Eubanks asked knowingly.

"Yes, I expect he will be willing to come with me."

"Very good, then, he shall keep an eye on you! I understand there is much trouble for a young man to get into in Wilmington!" The Reverend winked at Edward, and together, they laughed.

CHAPTER FOUR

"Wagon's ready to go," called Elijah over the din of activity on Moore's plantation. The planks that made up the flatbed were stacked high with choice timber from the far edge of one of the fields, carefully stacked and tied to the wagon for the journey to Wilmington. Elijah looked over the wagon one last time, clamping his hat down low on his head for a little relief from what was promising to be another hot day. Looking up, he noticed wisps of mares' tails in the clouds, a sure sign of wind and rain to come. He wanted to get an early start to beat the rain if they could.

Edward waved to him, signaling he was almost ready to go, but he was delayed by two of King's dogs nipping playfully at his feet as Edward waited for the approaching woman who carried a basket of food for their trip.

"Master Moore say for me to bring dis to you-- but you be sure to bring my sweet grass basket back, ya hear?"

"Yessum," Edward smiled and nodded as he took the pale green and sand-colored basket and tipped his hat to her. Cornelly was one of King's oldest slaves, and she just about ran the plantation, rumor had it. She had taken a liking early on to Edward, so she saw to it that he always had plenty to eat whenever she found him about the plantation. Today was no exception, judging by the weight of the basket.

He hurried to the wagon, joining Elijah who was already at the reins. With a swift "Yah" and a jolt, they were off.

The plantation's open greenway turned on to the sandy road that was the pride of Governor George Burrington. In addition to his own funds, he solicited other land owners and Parliament for monies to clear and maintain this road known as King's Highway as one of the main arteries through the growing provinces of North Carolina from Virginia to South Carolina. Every man in the state over the age of 18 was required by law to help maintain a portion of it, without compensation, unless they were operating or maintaining a privately owned ferry that was available for public use. Such a road system and ferries were available to man and beast to help commerce develop, and for a nominal fee, they were open to anyone wanting to travel well-defined paths through what would otherwise be thick timber land separated by the region's many smaller tributaries and creeks.

Edward and Elijah each had their turn at working on the roads for a period of a week earlier in the year, so they were exempt for the remainder of this year. During their stint, they made causeways by laying hewn logs in the desired direction of the road, spreading dirt on top, then icing the log and dirt pile with brush, small pine trees, and a final layer of dirt.

The day's travel was a mix of road and ferry, and could be made in a few hours' time, weather permitting. If the wind whipped up so the flatboard or barge ferries couldn't make it to one of the many landings available to travelers, the journey could take longer.

"Thanks for coming with me, Elijah. Since you've been up to Wilmington before, I figured you'd know the shortest route," Edward said as he and Elijah ducked under a low branch dripping with Spanish moss. From time to time, Edward pulled out a small satchel containing his charcoal and paper, and make quick sketches of what he saw along the way. He liked the way the Spanish moss--which wasn't really moss at all, but kin to the pineapple species--draped itself over just about anything, and grew at lengths that rivaled some of the elder men's beards he'd seen in church. While it looked lighter than air and soft, it actually had a sticky feel to it and it was home to biting insects like chiggers. Nevertheless, its silvery green threads still had an elegant look, Edward thought.

Elijah looked over at Edward's drawing. "You got a good eye, there. I never was much on writin' and drawin' and such." His leathery hands held the reins to Edward's gray mare loosely, and he yanked his straw hat down over the right side of his face to shield his eye from the morning sun. "You mind if we take a look at what Miss Cornelly packed in the basket? We got a mighty early start today, and I didn't make me a biscuit." He glanced in the general direction of the basket on the wagon's floorboard at Edward's feet.

"Good idea. I didn't get much of a chance to eat this morning, either." Edward put his paper and charcoal down on the bench between them, then pulled the basket up and drew back the cloth that covered a mix of cornbread, biscuits, and small chunks of ham. "Bless that woman," he said with a smile, as he passed a biscuit to Elijah. This was shaping up to be a grand day.

Sarah Jenkins was the only woman Edward saw as he entered the wharf's main office in Wilmington that windy July day. His first thought was that she looked so out of place. Standing with her back to a wall barely out of the wind, she held her deep green skirt in place against an updraft with one gloved hand and her pale green bonnet with the other. Despite the whirlwind of activities around her, she stood composed, straight, and beautiful.

Bustling about the warehouse were slaves carrying heavy cargo boxes and crates toward waiting ships, hawkers selling their wares of rum and food, and auctioneers seeing their charges walk down boarding planks to waiting owners and their chattel wagons. Yet she stood there, calmly soaking it all in: sights, smells, chaos.

Sarah's father seemed quite comfortable in the melee as he directed his foremen and other traders as they herded cattle and goods from ship to shore. Thaddeus Jenkins was the master of the wharf. As one of the top merchants in Wilmington, he owned a small fleet of ships plus the manpower necessary to handle them on their coastal trading routes. Atop each of his ships and his warehouse flew his personally designed flag: a gold arrow that pierced a thick circle set on a field of rich, dark green. Edward would later learn that this flag meant prosperity to Jenkins, and he liked to show if off as often as he could.

Jenkins' profits came from many sources. With his ships, he traded far to the north in Massachusetts and brought goods to the southern colony of Georgia. He also supplied the burgeoning colonial maritime traders with ship's stores, including pitch and tar from the region's long-leaf pines, and timber for framing new homes further to the south and the new western territories.

Edward almost lost sight of his goal of selling lumber to Jenkins when he saw Sarah. Gathering his confidence, he nodded in her direction, then approached Jenkins' high stand, and cleared his throat.

"Pardon me, Sir," Edward said, as he tapped on Jenkins' table.

Between shouting orders and checking in cargo, Jenkins looked up from his books, and peered at Edward over the top rim of his glasses. Appraising the young man, Jenkins straightened himself, and put down his quill.

"And what can I do for you, young man?"

"Sir, my name is Edward Marshall, and I've come from Brunswick to the south. We have a great deal of prime lumber that I am representing today. Perhaps you would care to see a sample that I have out in my wagon." Hopeful, Edward took a step away from the high table, and stole a glance in Sarah's direction.

It did not go unnoticed.

"Edward, you say your name is?" quizzed Jenkins. "As you can tell, we have plenty of lumber in this warehouse. I will, however, humor you. I could use a bit of fresh air. How about you, my dear?" He directed his question to Sarah. She stepped forward upon hearing her name. Her dark brown eyes met Edward's dead on, and she held her head up high. Edward was surprised and pleased all at once to learn that she was kin to Jenkins, and even more so that she accepted the invitation.

"Yes, Father, a bit of fresh air would be appreciated."

The threesome made their way through the crowd entering the warehouse and out onto the sandy street that fronted the river.

Elijah stood to one side of the long buckboard wagon, and when his gaze met Edward's, he hastened to pull forward two sample pieces of lumber that the pair brought specifically for the meeting. He then stepped away from the wood's end, and taking his hat in hand, turned his back.

"So you say this comes from down the road? In Brunswick?" Jenkins inspected the wood with his rough hands, looking down the wood's long edge at the cut and grain of the straight timber.

"Yes. We have some of the region's finest lumber available for shipbuilding and other needs. You might want to come take a look for yourself, when you have time to get a good look at everything." Edward quickly glanced in Sarah's direction, catching her eye and a flicker of a smile. He had partly intended to extend this invitation to her, and she seemed to understand.

"Well, Mr. ... what did you say your name is, fCatrine?" Jenkins looked Edward straight in the eyes, his hands never leaving the wood.

"Edward Marshall." He waited quietly.

"Well, Mr. Marshall, I think I will be coming to your town. This does look as though it would meet the needs of one of my buyers, a ship-builder of some repute. Perhaps you've heard of him, a Mister Layette. He comes all the way from Louisian' to purchase our woods, and a fair penny he pays, too. If I can get what I need for him, I will pay you a fair price," said Jenkins. "Let me run down your way toward the end of the month, and we will see what we can do."

"Very good. Perhaps ..." Edward hesitated. "Perhaps when you and your family come to visit, you will be so kind as to stay with me. I live in a small but comfortable cottage, and I would welcome you as my guests for as long as you wish to stay." Boldly looking at Sarah, Edward nodded as if willing Jenkins to commit to a visit.

Sarah opened her fan, bringing it to her fair face, but not so quickly that Edward missed her wide smile at his invitation. The wind caught her loosely draped peach shawl at once and blew it off of her arm, and he immediately turned to catch it. Elijah turned to help her as well, but bowed deeply and backed away when he saw Sarah agilely grab it before it touched the sand.

"You are as kind as you are shrewd," Jenkins said slyly. We will send word about our visit, and then we can discuss our quarters. For now, though, I must be getting back to the wharf. Come along, Sarah, it is about time for dinner." Obediently, Sarah began to follow in her father's path down the wide sandy street. But before she vanished into the sea of people, she turned around and curtsied to Edward, who tipped his hat at her. There was a brief meeting of eyes, and of smiles. Edward was pleased to have come all this way.

The ride home was a quiet one, with Elijah at the reins once outside of town limits. Edward, lost to his thoughts, did not notice the darkness of night creeping in, nor did he feel the pre-rain mist on his face. All he could feel was his heart pounding.

"She a pretty girl, ain't she?" Elijah piped up after some time. Edward nodded, but that was the extent of their conversation. Elijah smiled and kept the wagon moving. It would be early morning before they got back to Brunswick; he clicked in the direction of the horse, and progressed along the trail through the pines.

CHAPTER FIVE

In the weeks that followed, Edward received a hand-delivered note from Jenkins stating that he would be visiting soon. His words were clear and to the point: the purpose of his visit was to see lumber, dashing whatever hopes Edward had held regarding seeing Sarah. But if the trip were to be a success, then Edward would surely see Sarah again. He turned his attention to building a room for his guest, and upon consulting with the Reverend, Edward was able to secure supplies that he would need. He had hoped to finish the extra room onto his cottage prior to Jenkins' arrival, but Jenkins showed up on the docks a few days earlier than his note had indicated.

In fact, Edward would not have known about this early arrival in time, had it not been for Elijah. Carrying freshly forged nails from the foundry to the boatyard, Elijah noticed a small, green pilot schooner angling its way toward the town's main dock. One of its tanbark sails was tearing from along the luff, and all hands aboard were frantically trying to pull it down and keep it from tangling in the shrouds while navigating the shoal that lay just off the starboard side. All hands, that is, except one. Caught up by the sight, Elijah stood for a moment watching. A hard look at the motionless stout figure gave way to recognition, and Elijah ran to tell Edward of Jenkins' approach.

When he reached the boatyard, Elijah looked around for Edward. Matty nodded as Elijah approached, signaling toward the general direction where he last saw Edward. Elijah gave a partial smile and turned toward the back of the building, which was twice as large as a two-story barn.

With sweat pouring down his back, Edward was absorbed in his planking and did not hear Elijah coming. He stood on scaffolding a few feet off the dirt floor, hammering a square nail into the heart pine siding. Each piece of wood was positioned to overlap the one below it, and this lapped siding was soon caulked with pitch derived from the sap of abundant pines in the area. Even though each ship was built using similar techniques and supplies, each one carried its maker's distinctive mark. Edward's technique of notching the lapstrakes prior to adding them to the keel's bones helped hold a well of caulking--a technique that he felt would add years of life to his ships. The few boats that had left this very ramp with his technique were fine examples of craftsmanship Edward learned from master shipwrights, and he was eager to prove himself an equal. It was with such vigor that he set about to build every boat, regardless of size or purpose.

"You best get cleaned up," Elijah sighed. "Company coming." Elijah nodded toward the open doors that faced the river. Edward scampered down a ladder and dashed to the door, then quickly drew back inside when he saw who was approaching the wharf.

"He's early! I was not expecting him for two days," Edward quipped, quickly judging how long he'd have before Jenkins reached the dock. He hesitated only briefly as he took one more look, hoping that that Jenkins had brought his family--and Sarah in particular--along. Not seeing anyone else but Jenkins, he ran up the hill toward his cottage as fast as he could, mentally picturing how straight the place was and if he had a clean shirt to wear for this meeting. He bolted inside, snatching britches up off the bench and throwing them in a timbered box on the far side of his bed. Edward tore off his sweaty shirt and reached for a wash cloth in one hand and a fresh shirt in the other, spinning around to catch a glimpse of himself in the looking glass--disheveled, he struggled to wash and dress at the same time. Just as he finished washing his face, he made a mad dash for the docks. He slowed only when he saw Jenkins standing on the long-plank pier, watching his men tie the schooner fast to pilings.

"Mr. Jenkins," called Edward, raising his hand in welcome and trying hard to not appear winded.

"It seemed best for me to travel by boat," Jenkins explained to Edward once he reached the docks. "It has been awhile since I sailed these waters, and this kind weather made it seem a shame to come here any other manner."

"Well, that is a fine schooner you have, Mr. Jenkins. Fine lines, and a full compliment of sails--I wager she is a fast ship."

"Yes, she is that, it took only a day to reach you, though your waters are much more treacherous than in those surrounding Wilmington. There are shoals about the far side of the river and at the entrance there," he pointed out the spot where his boat had to jibe to avoid grounding--and the jibe tore the sail.

"I say, is there is a place we could have a meal? I got an early start this morning, and there is little aboard to eat this trip." Jenkins patted his round belly to emphasize his point.

"Mr. Jenkins, it would please me if you would come to my home and share supper with me," Edward said, extending his arm toward the general direction of his cottage. He had put away salt meat and biscuits only yesterday, so there would be enough for his guest, he hoped.

"No need to put yourself out … any of those taverns I see across the way will suffice. We can discuss what you have to offer over a meal." Jenkins looked back at his boat and then began marching ahead of Edward along Front Street toward the nearest tavern.

Daylight was still sufficient, and Edward wondered if there would be time to show Jenkins the available timber that Moore had set aside. The plantation was just a mile away, but he had yet to arrange for a buggy or wagon to see the goods. Edward scratched his head thoughtfully as he hurried to catch up with Jenkins.

"Mr. Jenkins, as I was unsure of your arrival, I have yet to schedule our visit to see the lumber that is available. It's just up the Brunswick River from here a little ways. Perhaps we can manage a visit tomorrow after you have rested from your travels."

"Edward, I have come prepared to purchase and carry what I find to my liking. I prefer we take my boat. That is why I traveled this way. There is very little I care less for than traveling by boat, but it seemed to make good sense, as it affords me a place to stay overnight without being a burden to you. Tomorrow, we shall board and head up river to see this supply of wood. If it is to my liking, my men will load it and we will be underway immediately after we conduct our business. You are representing the landholder, I presume."

"Yes, I am. The land belongs to Mr. King Moore, I believe you know him."

"Why that old coot. I was supposing it was him, when you first told me where you were from. Yes, yes, I know King. He is a fair man, so if he has fine lumber to sell, then I will surely buy it. We have had our dealings before, and to my recollection, they have been favorable."

Relieved, Edward blew out the breath he'd been holding. If there was to be a deal, then he would make his money, and he would have reason to call on Sarah in the future if King had other deals in mind with his friend in Wilmington.

The rest of the evening Jenkins and Edward got along well. Edward learned that Thaddeus Jenkins, his wife Isabel, and their daughter Sarah moved to Wilmington just a few years earlier from Annapolis, Maryland. Jenkins was successful in Annapolis as a merchant. He said that competition from other businesses in town was getting stiff as Annapolis' popularity grew, so he decided he would do well by being one of the first merchants in Wilmington. Isabel, he told Edward, was not keen on the idea of moving to "the backwoods", knowing that it lacked culture and fashion and the grand parties for which Annapolis was famous. But she soon grew to like the idea of being one of the grand dames of Wilmington's burgeoning society, and within a few years, was as busy as ever with activities that helped make the town a more delightful place to live--and a more profitable town for her husband, Jenkins winked.

Jenkins was not as forthcoming about his daughter as Edward would have hoped over supper, but he did not discourage Edward, either. By the end of the evening, Edward was at least sure that Sarah was not betrothed to anyone. He escorted Jenkins back to the wharf and to his schooner. A dim light could be seen hanging on deck, and one down below shined through a porthole. Aboard were two men, one man in a pale shirt and tattered pants working on the torn sail, and the other lounging against an oak barrel. His wide-brimmed hat was tilted on his bowed head, his arms crossed over his burley chest. He offered no help to his companion, and despite his apparent advancing years, his physique was that of a strong man.

"Many thanks to you, Edward, for the meal. We shall set sail with the tide, which the man there tells me is at dawn. Surely you know the tides here better than I do, so I will expect you here to guide us up the river."

"I assume your man knows these waters well. I will be here to offer any assistance I can," he said bowing slightly. "King Moore's plantation is off the main river and the passage is narrow. It is an easy sail from here. I will see you at dawn."

Edward watched Jenkins totter up the wooden ramp to his schooner, and then board with a little help from the man in the wide hat. Edward then headed back toward home. From the looks of the man Jenkins suggested was the captain, Edward was more settled in his answer as to why Jenkins thought better to not bring Sarah along.

In the morning, Edward hustled to the docks and greeted Jenkins, who was making his way from the boathouse.

"The door was not locked, so I decided to take a peek at what goes on in that building," he said, pointing to the boathouse. "That looks like a fine operation. Who owns these buildings?" His broad hand swept toward the waterfront's three structures.

"King Moore owns the boatworks there on the left. The building in the center is owned by the township, and to the right is another boathouse where we store supplies and build small craft."

"'We?'" You speak as if you know this business intimately," pried Jenkins.

"Ah, yes Sir, I do know it intimately. I am a shipwright. My hope is to finish my own ship soon for trade, when I can afford it. In fact, the extra money I earn is why I work odd jobs for King Moore."

"This is a good thing that you are enterprising," Jenkins approved. "Such a spirit will carry you far in these times. I gather than you are interested in more than boats, young man?" Jenkins finished buttoning his vest over his round belly, and pulled his felt hat down on a balding head.

Edward was unsure about Jenkins' question. Rather than answer, he began to point out the various shoals that could present problems as they left the docks, all while keeping an eye on the burly captain and his crew of one as they prepared the ship for departure. From the deck of Jenkins' ship, he could see an array of other ships, large and small, tied to the wharf as well as those anchored in the river, so navigating would be challenging.

Within a few minutes, they were underway and heading up the river toward Orton Plantation. When they sailed as far as they could, the crew lowered a fourteen-foot tender. Once Jenkins was in place, Edward climbed over the gunwale and down the rope ladder to the tender taking his place opposite of Jenkins. The captain stayed behind while the other man rowed the boat to the small landing at the edge of a finely manicured lawn.

This was Orton, a plantation carved out of marsh. Moore's home was humble as far as plantation manors went, but there were plans for the future. And, as it was, it was still grander than any home in Brunswick. The most important part of the plantation at this point was the rice and indigo fields in the marsh creeks that bordered the property. Off to the left of the landing was a stand of pine and sapling turkey oak trees. Further off were hardwoods, and stacks of lumber waiting to be bought and shipped off the property.

After surveying the lumber and discussing the particulars of price, Jenkins was satisfied that he was indeed getting a good deal.

"Just as I thought, King has something worth having. I think I shall take this off his hands."

He extended his hand to a very pleased Edward, who shook it vigorously. Then Jenkins' man began the arduous task of loading and ferrying the wood to the waiting ship. On the second trip back to shore, he brought with him the captain, who looked none too pleased with the prospect of hard labor. However, that was his charge, so he put his back in it, and soon the stacks were aboard the small schooner.

With the deal done, Jenkins took out his money sack from his belt, and handed money to Edward. After offering navigational advice, Edward thanked Jenkins again and offered to come to Wilmington for any projects that Jenkins might know of in the future. His goal, of course, was to see Sarah again, though he could not quite bring himself to ask permission to do so.

When they said their farewells, Jenkins made his way back to the small landing and aboard the tender, now heavily weighted with a few last pieces of timber. Edward saw them off, and as the schooner set sail, he headed toward King's office to give King his money.

He was greeted by three cocker spaniels nipping at his feet, jumping up for attention. Among his many endeavors, King was interested in breeding dogs. These three males were the beginnings of his efforts. King also had two female dogs, one in heat and the other already pregnant. It would be only a matter of time before King had puppies to sell to the fine people of neighboring cities ... like Wilmington, Edward thought. He would certainly ask for that assignment, to take the pups to waiting homes there as an excuse to call on Sarah. For now, he would have to be satisfied with earning his keep for this lumber deal.

King came to the door when he saw Edward coming, and the two discussed the day's transaction. King then offered Edward a seat while he went to his "counting room"--a special room separate from his office where he counted his money-- and returned shortly with a bag of it for Edward.

"Job well done, Edward. I am pleased you were able to clear the stock off my land, and that you got along well with Jenkins. We've dealt before, but I have been so busy here, I would not have had the time to be as social as the occasion would have dictated," explained King. "Besides, I understand he has a pretty young daughter about your age, I would guess," he added slyly. His knowing smile surprised Edward, who re-thought his words to uncover if he'd in any way hinted at his attraction to Sarah.

CHAPTER SIX

The man who accompanied Sarah's father on his journey was a little too curious about Edward, and Edward grew increasingly uncomfortable with his questions during frequent visits to Wilmington in the following months. King Moore had other sections of timber that would soon be ready for harvesting, and was eager to secure a buyer. While Edward was comfortable in presenting King's offer of timber to Jenkins, he was agitated at the sight of Ignatius Pell.

Pell clearly was a man of the sea, with years of wind and tide etched memorably on his ruddy forehead like so many lines on a treasure map. His pox-marked face and continence of an aging bully gave him an overall appearance of a man to be avoided.

Yet Pell persisted in making small talk with Edward. On each visit, he worked to draw a little more information out of Edward.

"How long you been in Brunswick?"

"You building ships, I hear tell."

"You a sailing man?"

"Is you akin to Master Moore, there?"

"I understand you to be partial to the preacher man-
-how long you been knowing him?"

"Where is your homeland, Sir?"

Seemingly inconsequential questions over the course
of many months, Edward thought. But one evening,
while riding south through the thick underbrush back
to Brunswick, Edward reflected that perhaps his answers
were not so disconnected. The hairs on the back of his
neck rose as he thought about Pell's possible motives. He
vowed to keep his own confidences from then on, and to
stop conversing with Pell.

Every visit to Wilmington under the guise of business gave Edward an opportunity to see the lovely Sarah.
He took advantage of his business dealings to extend
whatever time he was offered to stroll around the stately
grounds of the water view home on Fourth Street on the
edge of Wilmington proper. A grey stone building of two
stories, the structure housed residential quarters as well as
the business office of Mr. Jenkins. And with every visit,
Edward grew fonder of Sarah and more wary of Pell,
who always seemed to be about the property, tending to
a broken pump or mending a hen house. It was during
these visits that Pell approached Edward with one more
question, one more excuse for dialog. This day proved to
be no exception.

"Hey there, Master Marshall, I see you have brought
you a wagonload of timber to the waterfront this morning. I suspect there will be more to come, aye?" Pell lifted

his broad-brimmed hat slightly off his sweating brow, revealing a shiny forehead through ragged locks of black hair and small eyes squinting into the afternoon sun. He leaned carefully against a post of the porch that gave entry to Jenkins' office on the side of the house.

"Good afternoon, to you, Pell," Edward nodded slightly, as he mounted the stairs to the office, but stepped back to the street upon finding the office door locked. "Yes, I have just come from there, and am bound for Brunswick this evening, weather permitting." He rubbed his eyes and motioned to the darkening sky.

"I remember a storm off the coast of Barbados that kept me and the rest of a crew holed up in Bridgetown for seven days," Pell spoke barely above a whisper with his head down, looking at his hands as if reading a book. He was half turned toward Edward, and the mention of the port sent a chill down Edward's back. "It weren't too bad, though, our ship's master paid us out of his own pocket while we waited. He was keen to leave the harbor in a hurry, so he kept us paid so we would be on the ready to leave once that storm cleared."

"Did you sail often out of Barbados?" Edward's voice quivered, as he tried to camouflage his interest.

"From time to time. It really weren't never up to me, but to the captain of whichever ship I sailed on. This particular captain--if you could call him such--was eager to leave, see, but not too keen on coming back. Seems he had his reasons."

Hoping it was just idle conversation, Edward sought to take his leave gracefully so that he could make his way toward home. But before he could get away, Pell cornered him:

"You are from there, Barbados, yes?"

"I do not call that port my home, Sir," Edward said stiffly.

"Perhaps I am mistaken, but you remind me of someone I met many a year ago. You look as though you could be her relations. In fact, you are the spittin' image of this woman, perhaps though a little fairer, or her ghost come to haunt me. But that was a much different time, Sir. A much different time. I don't necessarily blame you if you prefer not to claim that heritage, but there is secrets you could know about your mother and your father, if you were so related...which you say you are not."

"I've said nothing of my heritage, Sir, and I've no more to say to you on this subject. Good day." Edward shoved his hat on his head and stormed away from the porch as efficiently as he could. He felt his neck grow hot, and quickly mounted the seat of his empty wagon. He was off with a terse "Yah" to his gray mare, and headed down the sandy street toward the waterfront. This Pell was hinting. He was fishing for information, and Edward was terrified of what a disclosure could mean.

A month passed between visits to Wilmington. Yet Edward nearly dreaded the next visit, and what unexpected questions Pell might have for him.

But dread was tempered by desire to see Sarah again. With each visit, he would strive to spend with her as much time as he could without raising her father's suspicions.

During some of their visits, the two strolled through the streets together, watching the commotion of a growing city. An occasional conversation took place in the Jenkins' home, but the pleasant weather of fall beckoned them outside to a rose garden in the rear of the house. They were proper meetings, filled at first with polite conversations, and an ever watchful Isabel Jenkins rocking on the porch knitting. But polite conversations gradually gave way to shared thoughts about what the future might hold. Edward told Sarah of the progress of his boat building, and destinations he would like to sail to--places he'd read and dreamed about. Sarah seemed keen to travel, too, and had seen many towns further north with her parents. She said she was fond of the idea of traveling on the water, because of the different view of the land and wildlife it afforded.

"When I was younger, I loved to play at the edge of the Severn River and watch the boats coming and going from the harbor, or rocking at anchor," Sarah explained. "I love the motion of sails filled with wind--so graceful, so peaceful--I just always thought I would like to go sailing, too. My father, as you might have guessed, is not the least bit interested in boats, and my mother, well, the only rocking she ever wants to do is in that chair on the porch!" Sarah giggled and turned away from the porch so her mother could not see her expression.

Edward did all he could to stifle his laugh.

"Do you miss it? Annapolis, I mean. Your father told me that there were lots of parties to go to, and much to do."

"Sometimes I miss going to the theater or to the festivities that happen just before the horse races for which Annapolis is famous. Mother likes to go twice a year, so I join her and we have a nice time. Now that I am nineteen years old, though, it is just not the same anymore. I think of Annapolis differently than I did as a young girl. Now there is more pretense, and more visitors. It is just not the same," Sarah looked off to the water.

"Would you ever want to live there again, Sarah? I mean, now that you are a young lady, surely you can go wherever you choose."

"I know I can, but I haven't decided if I want to go anywhere else, yet. Wilmington is growing, and as a one of the first businessmen to arrive, my father has developed a strong position. I think I might want to help him run one of his businesses if he will let me. My mother, on the other hand, wants me to marry well, and marry soon, so that I can give her a grandchild." Sarah smiled slyly.

Edward blushed.

"What other businesses does your father run, besides brokering wood?" Edward tried to regain his composure.

"He owns a sawmill, so he buys wood to mill and sell to people who want to build their homes. He also sees the need for shipwrights in this town, so he runs a company of shipbuilders that he "rents" out for wages at the boatyard on the waterfront. He is a developer, building homes and building the warehouses and docks that support the shipbuilders. And I think you know that he owns several ships of his own, and uses them to trade with colonies to the north."

Sarah sat down on a small wooden bench, adjusted her billowing robin's egg-blue skirt around her, and continued. "We moved here to start the new community, and to take advantage of its newness. Father often calls it the 'next Annapolis', and wanted to capitalize on the city's location on a major water system that can carry goods further inland on the Cape Fear River, south the other colonies, or east to the islands."

Edward hesitated, "do you think he will let you run any of his businesses someday? I mean, if that is what you want?"

Sarah looked up at him thoughtfully before answering. "I sometimes think that is the path I should try to follow, if he will let me. I don't know if he would let me take over any of his business ventures, as he is a bit old-fashioned; but to be truthful, more than anything, I enjoy meeting the families that sail in and out of the harbor on all manner of boats. I enjoy listening to them tell their stories of sailing together, and I wish…I wish I were able to sail to faraway ports with someone I love, and live my days on the water." It was Sarah's turn to blush for sharing such personal thoughts.

But Edward reserved his expressions of feelings, and changed the conversation again. Talk about the weather, talk about the boats, talk about anything but this, he kept telling himself. The afternoon shadows grew long, and after a bit more conversation, Edward said goodbye and made his way to his horse tied to the post in front of the house.

"It is too soon for me to feel so strongly about her," Edward confided in his friends Matty and Richard when he returned to Brunswick. "We only met a few months ago. I mean, I enjoy her company when we visit every few weeks, but how long should I call on her before I know she's…you know, right for me? It's too soon, isn't it?"

Richard gave his signature belly laugh. "You can never tell when Fate comes to call. Sometimes, you are just destined to fall, even if you think it's too soon. Boy, when I was your age, I had already tied the knot--and the noose around my neck with it!"

"Don't frighten him, man," Matty chimed. "Not everyone feels the way you do about the state of holy matrimony."

"Holy or un, it is not a state I wish to revisit. No, a bachelor should stay a bachelor for as long as he can, Mate, for in the end, it's your friends you count on, not your wife." Richard spat on the ground as his said this, and turned his attention back to his hammer.

Between advice and jabs, the three focused their efforts on the ship in the cradle. Made of heavy pine and oak timbers, the pilot schooner they were working on had taken them the better part of a year to complete. In its finished state, the schooner had a bow similar to that of a clipper, with a long head and sharp angles to the sides. Because the coastal waters were shallow, the pilot schooner design called for a moderate draft of no more than seven feet, good for the narrow, changing channels of the coastline on which it sailed. Rigging would be raked back, a traditional schooner rig some might say, with a headsail rig, a small foresail, and a large main. A small, raised deckhouse was fitted with roof-top transoms and opening portholes for natural light and ventilation, and there was room on deck for storage of one long shore boat measuring twenty to twenty-five feet in length, or two smaller coastal boats averaging fourteen to fifteen feet in length. These smaller boats would be lowered to the water as tenders for crew and cargo with the assistance of a mast or boom tackle. One of the distinguishing features of the schooner was its low freeboard. This low freeboard showed the head of the rudder, and the overall length of the vessel they were building was sixty-six feet.

The *Virginia* as she was to be called was a fine craft, and everyone who had a hand on it was looking forward to her completion in December.

"Just go with what you feel, Edward," Matty said after giving it much thought. "If this young woman seems like someone you could come home to every night, then that's not an entirely bad situation. If she is interested in what you want for your future, and you think she could help you to reach your goals, then by all means, continue to call on her. And being related to one of the biggest merchants in Wilmington could be a big help to you when you start looking for cargo to haul."

"I personally would haul myself away before I met up with another marriage," Richard said lowly. "Tain't nothing worse than wanting to go to sea and having a wife to hold you back. When I was coming up, we all went to sea. It was rough on my mother, I tell you. Think twice before you push in that direction, if your heart is on the water."

"Richard, I think Sarah is of a mind to go sailing." Edward didn't want to go into it any further, so he turned his attention back to his task.

"Maybe so. Maybe not. Sometimes, the reasons people do and say things is not because they mean them. Just remember that the next time the two of you talk." Richard spat again, and walked away.

Mulling it over, Edward wondered if he really knew Sarah's desires. He would have to weigh her answers carefully before he made a commitment to her in his own heart.

CHAPTER SEVEN

During his monthly trips to Wilmington, Edward called on Sarah. Yet November's visit proved different from the rest, as Sarah was unavailable when he was announced to her. Standing with hat in hand in the foyer of the great marble tiled hall, Edward was not quite sure whether he should leave, or stay and see Mr. Jenkins about King Moore's latest harvest of pine sap and timber.

To Marna, Sarah's West Indies servant, Edward half whispered. "I will trouble Miss Jenkins for only a moment, but I really would like to see her," Edward hesitated.

"Sir, Miss Sarah is not ready to see no men folk right now, she is busy. I tell her you been here." Marna crossed her arms and waited patiently for Edward to leave the foyer, a sly smile coming to her round chocolate face. Beaten, Edward nodded to her, and turned toward the oak door. Before he reached it, Sarah called out to him from the top of the stairs.

"Edward!" She caught her breath at the sight of Marna, but slowly descended the curved stairs, her pale complexion made even paler by the contrast of her deep burgundy dress. With each step closer, she grew more composed, more dignified, if not more distant.

However radiant, she looked small and frail today, thought Edward. Perhaps she is not feeling well?

"Edward, thank you for waiting," Sarah stated quietly, showing him to the side parlor. Decorated in hues of blue, green and amber, the parlor was often the secluded meeting room of Edward and Sarah during his visits, where they could talk without a chaperone, as long as the door remained open.

"Sarah, are you not feeling well today? I was concerned when Marna said you wouldn't see me."

"Edward, it is not a question of my health, really, that kept me from seeing you but a concern."

"Please tell me."

Sarah drew in her breath, and then spoke. "Please do not interrupt me before I am done, for I may not get the courage to speak this boldly with you again." She pointed to a tufted chair, and took a seat on a small settee opposite from Edward. "In the months that we have been visiting, not once have you expressed your intentions to me, or to my father. And he feels that if you were interested in pursuing courtship, you would have already spoken your mind to him. While it is not my place to tell you how you feel, or how you should act upon your feelings, I can only account for my own. I am certainly fond of you, Edward. Yet my father feels that it is time for me to allow other gentlemen to call whom he feels have promising futures. I am obliged to listen to his wishes as long as I am under his roof, but I do not have to like it. He has asked that at the end of this year, if you have not spoken of your affection for me, that I must ask you to stop calling. It pains me to think that I might not enjoy your company again, but my father is interested in my well being. I am about to turn twenty and, as a woman, I need to be mindful of my future."

Edward was stunned. Taking in what she had said, he wasn't sure where to begin. He stood and took a step toward her. "If I may speak now …"

"No, you may not," Sarah flustered, holding out her hand to stop him from speaking or progressing toward her. "I am not finished yet, and what I have to tell you is very important. A Mr. Patrick Monahan has come to call on me. He lives here in Wilmington, and is from a family of means. He has made his intentions known to my father, and my father is quite in favor of my seeing him during the holiday season. He would like me to accompany him to the Christmas Ball at the Winslow plantation, and I have yet to give him my answer. I have been waiting for you to invite me yourself, but as you seem slow to know about the events of this city, I felt it necessary to tell you, in case you wanted to invite …."

Sarah was cut short by Edward's kiss--he darted at her and kissed her squarely on her lips, then hastily backed away, fearing the worst. But Sarah remained silent much longer than he anticipated. He sat down next to her gingerly and held out his hand to hers. She smiled, dazed, and gave him her hand.

"Sarah, it is right for you to speak your mind, and tell me how you feel. I would not want it any other way. In all the months we've been visiting, I have certainly enjoyed your company. I understand your father's concern about my intentions. If I had a daughter as lovely as you, I would want her to marry well so that she would be taken care of in a befitting manner." He took a deep breath, and continued.

"My intentions are to call on your father and to inquire if I may court you properly. I had not wanted to rush this, because I feared my status as a broker for King Moore would mar his judgment of me as a proper suitor. I have been slowly putting away wages, and am building my own small ship. As I have mentioned to you earlier, I have plans to be a merchant shipper. At first, with only one ship, profits will be slow to come, and I felt it might be better for me to prove myself in this venture before I asked to court you. At most, it will take me until the summer until my ship is complete. King Moore has indicated that he will sponsor my venture for its first two years, and I will make good on what has been so generously offered to me. If you will allow me to, I will speak with your father now, and if my request is rejected, please understand that I will continue to call on you, regardless of your father's wishes.

"Certainly, I would be honored if you would accompany me to the Christmas Ball, though I have not received an invitation myself, nor do I have the proper attire for such an event. As it is an important affair for your community, and quite probably for your father, I understand the urgency with which you are pressed. While you assuredly may accompany any man of your choosing, if you will allow me five days, I will make inquiries. If at the end of five days' time you have not heard from me on the matter of the Ball, you will at least know that I am unable to escort you. Is that a fair request?"

Sarah nodded.

"Very good, then. Please accept my thanks for seeing me this afternoon, and for speaking your mind. A woman should have the right to such open conversation with the man who expects to be her husband," smiled Edward, as he patted Sarah's hand. He stood up, pulled her to her feet, and gently raised her hand to his lips. After he made a quick bow, he smartly turned on his heel to leave.

Sarah stood motionless in the parlor. "I will be waiting to hear from you in five days, Edward. Thank you for your efforts." She smiled at him, as he tipped his hat and left.

Edward glided out the door and across the porch, his mind reeling at what just happened. His brashness surprised him. Sarah was just as surprised. And pleased, he thought. They were of like mind, he knew. It was just a matter of timing. He made his way from the main house to the side entrance of Mr. Jenkins' office, but Jenkins door was locked. Edward decided to head to the waterfront warehouse to look for him, and started to make his way on foot down a side alley toward the water.

It was a short walk these few blocks, and the day was clear. Only one purpose clouded his way: how to ask Mr. Jenkins for the proper time to court his daughter. He wondered if indeed he could arrange for an invitation to the Ball, and then there was the matter of proper clothes. Perhaps King would be able to help, or even Eubanks ….

"Hail, Edward!" An all too familiar, raspy voice broke Edward's revelry. Pell stood partially hidden by shadows in a doorway just ahead. He spat openly on the cobblestone street, and tipped a broad-brimmed crusty hat in Edward's general direction. Pell was the last person Edward wanted to run into today, and he felt robbed before even speaking to Pell.

"Say, Edward, I had a hunch you would be heading to the waterfront today. Perhaps you would care to join me for a drink before you continue on?" Pell had one foot in the doorway of a small dark tavern, a place that Edward would have walked past had it not been called to his attention in this manner.

"Thank you, no, Pell. I have no time to spare today." Edward tried to brush him off politely, and continued on his way.

"Too bad, Mate. I have run across some interesting information that might further your designs on the Lady Saray and your shipbuilding efforts, but, tsk, you seem never to have the time."

Edward froze. Turning and seeing the ragged man's expression, he flew at Pell with a raised fist. "How dare you even mention her name? You are not worthy to even look at her, you filthy ...."

"There, there, Chap, I meant nothing by it, Pell said, dodging the blow. "I gather that she is your intended ... or that you would like her to be, and I only want to help you. I feel I owe it to you."

"Owe me? You owe me nothing, man. I have no obligation to you, either." Edward regained his composure, stood up straight, and began to walk away.

"Ah, but I feel as though I <u>do</u> owe you. But if you are not willing to hear me out, Sir, then that is your affair. I only was trying to help."

Curious now, Edward faced Pell. "What, pray tell, do you know that would be of any use to me? I have nothing from you, and I believe you have nothing on me. Am I mistaken?"

"Perhaps you would care to join me in a drink. Come on, then. This is a discreet place, and I won't tell a soul you come to share a table with the likes of me."

Edward hesitated a moment, but decided that he would hear Pell out. He followed Pell in through the heavy scarred oak door.

Edward's eyes took a moment to adjust to the darkness. Thick stone walls permeated with the smells of years of whiskey and smoke filled his nostrils, and the mud and straw floor was sticky from one too many spills. Hearty laughter came from darkened corners of the room, and men of various sizes, ages, and descriptions shared planked tables and benches.

Pell motioned for him to follow toward a bench and table shoved up against the wall. A small lantern lit a path between tables, and Edward clutched his hat in one hand and held the other one by his side at the ready in case he needed to use it. Not accustomed to such places, Edward was taken aback by the overwhelming smell of body odors mixed with stale smoke and rotten food. This was a place where Pell was very much at home, Edward thought. And these were his comrades. While they were all different in their looks and nationalities, they shared a common feature: they all looked worn and tired.

"There, have a seat ... if you like," Pell was uncharacteristically polite as he pulled the heavy wooden planked table away from the wall for Edward to slip behind.

The idea of keeping his back to the wall seemed like a good one, considering the clientele, Edward thought.

"Now what is your pleasure? Rum? Ale?" He flagged the tavern master who leaned with his back against a plaster and horsehair wall, one foot up on a bench, and a pewter mug in his hand. He was a jovial sort of fellow, red-faced and balding, with fat spilling out of his shirt and over his tan britches. The tavern master glance saw Pell's waving hand, and he ambled toward the table.

"I see you have no mug, Sir. What will you have?"

"Ale."

"Coming, Mate." The tavern master waddled back to his post and heartily sang out for ale. A young boy whom

Edward guessed to be about age seven brought it to the table. Yet even at his tender age, his mannerisms were that of an experienced chap. While he was watching the boy stride confidently through the rough crowd back to the bar, Edward felt the weight of Pell's stare on him.

"This is not a social visit, Pell," Edward said looking Pell squarely in the face. "You suggest that you know information that could be useful to me. You have my attention for as long as I have ale in my glass."

"Ah, that will be plenty long enough, I assure you. First of all, let me tell you that I mean you absolutely no harm. In fact, your dislike for me should be enough of a warning to keep me away from you, but there's this ... well, this past that we share, though I don't think you are aware of it.

"Many, many years ago when I was a man of the sea, I happened upon the island of Barbados. Now mind you, I was a much younger man in those days and looking for adventure, you might say. That was in 1717. Well, there I was, in Bridgetown, in a waterfront tavern not too different from this one here. I overheard a man, a fancily dressed man I might add, boast that he would pay good wages to any man willing to accompany him on a sailing adventure. Seems he had a sloop in the harbor, and needed crew. I was in need of an adventure as much as in need of wages, so I jumped up and offered my hand to him. It didn't take long for a crew to be rounded up, and we was to set sail as soon as the weather cleared ... about a week later, I think it was. It was rare that the likes of me was *actually paid* before setting sail, and this bloke was doing that, and more."

"I moved my few belongings on board that very day, and that ship was a fair and fast ship, to be sure. It had ten pieces of artillery on the gun deck, and she was named the *Revenge,* though I know not why. There was seventy of us all together he paid. That was a lot of wages that came from his very own pockets. But by him paying us as he did rather than having us sign a contract like I had to do on other ships, well, we let him have his way a bit once we learned the truth about him as a captain.

"I heard tell of a story about him. Now, I don't claim to know the truth behind much of it, but I can tell you what I did learn to be true. Our captain was not a sea-faring man. He was a gentleman, a man of good breeding and some schooling. He had one of the largest sugar plantations on the island of Barbados, and at his age, he should have been content to enjoy his good fortune there. He was high society, see. But that weren't enough for him, I reckon, as he bought this ship. Rumor was that he had bought the ship for trading with other islands there in the Caribbean, and I guess his society friends believed him. But we heard another story: he wanted to go to sea, I was told, to escape his wife. She was meaner than most men on that boat I heard, though I never met her. Let me think … we had a little ditty about her:

"Oh, the wife she is a-calling, but he won't be answering

the wife she is a-looking, but he won't be found.

Oh, the wife she is a shrew, but he is smarter still

the wife she is a shrew, but he is smarter still."

"Ah, but I digress. Our captain, he was a dandy. He wore ruffles and hosiery at first, and even carried a walking stick for first few days of our voyage. He had jewelry that put most ladies to shame, and I tell you, we was all fed and treated well by him. When asked by one of us about our course, he was secretive about our destination, which always adds to an adventure. The queer thing about the start of our voyage was that he insisted that we leave in the middle of the night. This is unusual because of the reef that protects the harbor, and in our sea-faring tradition, a bad omen. But leave before sunrise we did.

"And we was not long out of the harbor before it was made known to us that a woman was aboard--and not our captain's wife, either, if you get me meaning. She was a red-haired lovely, she was. I for one was glad to have something as lovely to see on board that ship. All the rest of the crew, well, they looked much like me, I suppose. Anyway, she had eyes that a man never forgets: pools of steely blue on this Frenchie, and fair skin paler than the sands of Barbados." At this, Pell looked directly at Edward, and pointed his long fat finger at Edward's own dark blue eyes, to emphasize his point.

"Anne Marie. That was her name. She was a fine looking, kind-hearted woman, too. Her presence aboard may have been a distraction, and a good one for the captain me thinks, because we did not see much of the two of them for most of our voyage to the Carolina coast. Our captain wanted to show her one special place, and then return her to Barbados where he felt she would be safer than at sea. We made our way to the river not too far south from here, right below your own Brunswick, and anchored out on the island. Smith Island it is called. Have you been there?" Pell took a long swallow from his mug.

"I have been there to fish in the backwaters behind the island, yes."

"Well, perhaps the next time you go, you shall visit this spot that I know of so well. It is where our captain and his lady made camp, and stayed nearly a fortnight. It was none too sheltered, not like the backwaters and creeks you have fished, but it is wildly beautiful. The lady was content there. I was enlisted as their boatswain. Not only was I entrusted with keeping the other crewmen in line while aboard our ship, I also toted their camp gear to and from the ship. I set up their camp, and helped to cook meals. I even was there when he ... but I am getting ahead of meself. I shall come back to that part of the story in a minute."

Edward listened intently, quite forgetting about his ale.

Pell continued. "Many months passed, and we made way for waters north, setting course for the Virginia Capes. Along the way, we took several ships. Do you know what I mean by that, Edward?"

"_Took_? Do you mean that you commandeered another ship?"

"Exactly. We took all the cargo, which was good thing because there was some well-provisioned ships from a northern colony, if memory serves. Most ships were loaded with guns and cannon, and we took what we wanted, and set them adrift. The crew had the choice to join us, or not. Most chose to join our crew, and we made our way along the coast until we found another ship worth taking. Our captain had never done this sort of thing before, mind you, but this is why he wanted to go to sea. He wanted to go a-pirating, and with each ship mastered, he gained more confidence. He even took to burning ships from Barbados, as if to cover his trail, or maybe send a message back to his wife, we jested. The first ship he burned was named the *Turbes*. I remember watching her burn to the waterline, thinking that was such as waste of a good ship. Most pirates during those days would have made her a second ship in a fleet, but not our captain. No, he had a mind of his own (some say he was a bit touched, but I cannot comment on that). I remember one ship in particular, there was fine ladies aboard, and our captain let them keep their wedding bands and finery, so he got the name "gentleman" pirate. In a manner of speaking, he was that already, as he was a man of letters."

"Anyway, we sailed further north to New England, but found the climate to his disliking, so we returned to southern waters around here and to Smith Island, so his lady could rest, and then back to the islands, to Barbados, as he had promised his beloved. It was there, that my tale grows sad."

"Pell, this is all very interesting, but what is it to me but a tale? If you have something to tell me …." Edward was growing impatient.

"Ah, yes, well, the tale is in the telling, man. As I was saying, the lovely Frenchie soon needed to be put ashore. It was to be a joyous returning, but Fate had something else in mind. I helped the captain carry his lady to a small white chattel house with a red roof that sat on top of tall rock cliffs on the eastern side of the island, where she would give birth to a son. But she did not live past the moment to see him but for a short while. Our captain was so tore up about it, he called for a preacher man to marry them right then and there. I do not think the preacher man made it to the cottage in time, nor do I think he wanted to perform the ceremony, but when a dagger is held to yer throat…" Pell made a motion of a dagger being held to his neck, and shrugged his shoulders. "What a sad day. I was not sure then why he did it, but he made us take his lady back aboard, and we left that little bundle of a boy with a Negro woman on the island."

Edward's blood ran cold. He could see his hands on the table in front of him, but he did not recognize them as his own. In a split second, he realized the man across from him was telling the truth, and that his secret was known. He looked up at Pell, who was talking faster now. Edward tried to imagine Pell a younger man, carrying a lifeless body to a ship. He imagined Pell walking several steps behind a sad pirate, respectful of the tragedy.

"From there, we sailed back to this coast, and after one last trip to Smith Island to put the lady to rest at her favorite spot under a gnarled tree that grew wild on an open dune, we prowled the sea for the better part of a year, I think it was.

"Then we met up with Blackbeard in the Bay of Honduras. That was an odd arrangement, but I recall that Blackbeard came aboard about the time that the crew was growing weary of our captain's antics. Blackbeard was sailing aboard his *Queen Anne's Revenge*, and the two enjoyed each other's company and decided to plunder ships together. Blackbeard soon double-crossed our captain and commandeered the faster *Revenge*, locking the captain in quarters below deck aboard his own *Queen Anne's Revenge*. We was then under the command of a Mr. Richards who was stern with us, but he had our confidence quickly, and we shaped up."

"I heard our captain thought he finally convinced Blackbeard to give him back his ship, and the two discussed retiring from pirating in favor of the Governor Charles Eden's offer of pardon which would allow them to live on the spoils of their voyages wherever they chose.

"But while our captain sailed to Bath at the mouth of the Pamlico to the north of here to take advantage of the Governor's kind pardon, Blackbeard took over our ship again and looted the cargo hold, taking with him all of our booty, and sailed us to Charleston. Well, I have to wager our captain was mightily upset when he learned of the double crossing. When he finally found us, he grew mean. After he took on the town of Charleston by robbing ships in port, he sought after Blackbeard with a vengeance. I am glad to say we never did catch up with the bastard; he was evil to his core. No, after we captured another ten or twelve ships, we met our voyage's end nearly where you make your home now." He hesitated, and took a long drink. "I do not know how much more I should tell you. You are looking pale."

"Go on." Edward tightened his grip around his mug. His stomach turned as he imagined what was to come next.

"Very well, then. Like I was saying, we was in the waters just south of here on the Cape Fear River. The ship, she was careened in the shallow waters at low tide so we could clean her hull. I can show you the spot next time I come to Brunswick. At that point, we was feeing rather invincible. Foolishness on our parts, I suspect.

"But we was caught by one Colonel William Rhett of Virginia. I did not learn this until later, but he was hired by the good people of Charleston to rid the waters of pirates. I heard how he set out after the pirate Charles Vaughn, but found us instead. Unfortunately for Rhett, his boat ran aground, and our two ships lay with their cannons pointing at the sky. When the tide came back in, Rhett captured us after a ferocious battle where I lost forty-two of my crewmates. He took us back to Charleston, towing our ship.

"At first, we was all held in the Provost Dungeon in the Exchange Building. Then a few days later, the captain was moved to the Sheriff's house. While he was there, he made friends with the sheriff, and he was a prisoner in name only. He became a society man, it seemed, and he was living the high life again. Late one night, a slave helped him escape. Our captain was dressed as a woman, I have to tell you, and he was rowed to a beach just across the harbor in a small tender. I never did learn how he found the slave's confidence, but I do know that he was bound to stay a pirate rather than fall back into the civility that the people of Charleston wanted to share with him.

"Once again, Rhett quickly recaptured him. This time, our captain he was thrown in prison, and while he was there, I'm told he wrote a pathetic letter of repentance addressed to the Governor, begging for his life. Needless to say, it didn't work, and he was tried along with most of his crew by Sir Nicholas Trott, Esquire, the judge of the Vice-Admiralty Court. Our captain was hung on December 10, 1718, at the waterfront. His body was then tarred and left to dangle for four days as a reminder to other would-be pirates, and he was buried in the marshes at the end of the peninsula."

"How is it that you escaped from such a fate?" Edward quizzed.

"I was granted a pardon because I gave the Governor information about ships we looted and where some of the treasure was stored. He set me free with a promise to kill me if he ever caught me in Charleston again. As you can imagine, I stayed well away from that town ever since, and have kept to meself here in Wilmington helping merchants such as Mr. Jenkins for many a year.

"But of course you realize that this is more than a story of a young man's adventure, yes?"

Edward stared at him squarely.

"You know I am speaking of your father, now, Edward?"

It was the question Edward knew was coming, and he dreaded it. "Yes, Pell, I know of whom you speak. But for the life of me, I know not how you've made this connection. When I left Barbados, I was a boy."

"There is one thing I shall never forget: the deep blue of her eyes, your mother's. And her pale skin topped by that dark red hair, exactly the same color as yours. You favor her so much, that I recognized her in you the first day I saw you on the wharf in Brunswick. I thought you was her ghost coming to haunt me for what I did. Anyway, I did a little asking about, learned of your arrival here as a young boy in the care of the good Reverend. Then, I did some more figuring and asking about, and learned that the ship you came on was from Barbados. From there, it was not too far a stretch for me to remember enough and reach the conclusion that you *are* Major Stede Bonnet's son."

Edward was shocked at his reaction upon hearing that name. It was if a ghost had slapped him in the face, and yet there was relief at knowing about his past: his mother, *and* his father. In one sudden moment, he wanted to know everything he could about both of them. All of it, good and bad. Pell was not going to disappoint him, either. For the next two hours, Pell recounted what he knew of Edward's lineage, and filled in the missing pieces of a puzzle that Edward had shelved expecting never to be interested in it again.

Tied in with this interest in his past was concern for his future: what would Sarah say if she knew he was the son of a pirate and a whore?

"I can see that my story is only part news to you, Edward," Pell's voice broke Edward's thoughts. "Perhaps you wonder why I would bother to tell you all of this now?"

Edward cocked his head and looked at Pell. Pell was getting on in years, his etched face chiseled by time in the sun and wind. His clothes, though old, were not too tattered to resemble their former style. Clearly, Pell had money at one time.

"Do tell me. Why now? You have had this knowledge for quite some time, I gather."

Leaning close enough for Edward to smell the stench of his breath, Pell smirked, "It should not be difficult for a man of your background to understand that a little gold can go a long way. I am, as you surely have noticed, too old to work for long bouts, yet I do what little must be done to keep myself fed and in ale. That is how I happened to be with Mr. Jenkins. He is a good man, a bit of a miser, though. I would like to have a bit more to rely on in my old age, see? When I was younger, I knew how to get aboard a ship to just about any destination I desired.

But these days, merchant masters prefer younger, stronger men than me. Or they want fare for passage. I have a hankering to go back to Barbados. I was figuring, as you have a ship that is close to complete, well perhaps you would like experienced crew and a navigator who knows them waters well.

"Now, you are shaking your head. I understand you have no reason to help me return to that island, and I can see that you do not much care for the likes of me either. You are entitled to your opinions, man. But listen to me: I happen to know the whereabouts of a stash of gold and jewels that might see me through my old age if I remain in Bridgetown, and I would be willing to share it with you, reserving the smaller portion for meself, of course. Certainly, that would be worth the price of passage. And it would help you in establishing yourself as a proper shipwright and provider for the lovely Miss Sarah." He sat back in his chair, looking content for making his offer.

Edward took in the proposal. "You said several hours ago that you felt obliged to help me, but you have not said why you feel you have this debt."

"Oh, yes, I was getting to that. You see, it has to do with the stash I mentioned, and with your poor mother. She was with us as we captured several ships, and quite frankly, I think seeing that may have made her weak in her distress. One evening, while I was carrying away her food as she rested in her quarters, I happened upon a small trunk that your father had put aside for her. A small case filled with gold and jewels and the like lay open for me to see, as if the Major had just presented it to the lady. I am guessing that its' contents was to keep her in style when she returned to the island. I do believe he meant well, and wanted for her to have this small fortune to help raise you once he realized that she was in the family way. Whether he planned to return to her, I do not know. But Barbados was her home, and she had her people there, so I suspect he felt he was doing the right thing by her."

"Anyway, in addition to carrying her to the cottage on the cliffs that day you was born, I also lugged trunks of clothes and trinkets that we had ... taken ... to that little place. I put it all in a small shed to the back of the property that was built into the cliff, and was told to by the Major to give an accounting of their contents to the Mistress's nurse, who met us at the shore. Well, I did that. I told her of all the contents of the trunks ... except one."

"The one with the case of jewels and gold?" Edward asked, unsurprised.

"Yes, except that one. While your father was tending to her and dealing with the preacher man, I was out back in that little shed digging for all I was worth, and stashing that little case in a hole under the floorboards. It was not a deep hole, but just deep enough to hide it."

Edward leaned back in his chair and rubbed his eyes. The dark room's smoke was thick and he was tired.

"So you feel obliged to share with me my 'inheritance' ... for a fee?"

"Exactly. I think it a fair trade. I have been meaning to get back there for years, and have been cast off ships because of my age or … well, I might as well tell you. I have a liking for grog."

"I see. And what makes you so sure that this case is still there, after all these years? Surely the land is owned by new owners, or it has been discovered by now."

"I had been thinking the same thoughts as you, and was counting myself bound for the potter's field, when only two months ago, I ran into a man that I used to know in Bridgetown who had recently made his way to Wilmington. As we got reacquainted and talked of the old days, he told me a tale about a place where he had floundered after a long night in St. Phillips Parrish on the east side of the island. He told me of how he nearly lost his life on the cliffs that overlooked a lovely strand of sand and palm trees there. That part of his story sparked my interest. He said that there was a woman, a kindly old woman and her old darkie, who took him in to her cottage which was an expanded chattel house with a red roof. She fed him in the morning. As we soon discovered, we was talking about the same beach, the same cliffs, and the very same house. I guess it must have looked much the same as it was when I was there. When we was there. I began to realize that there was a good chance then that the case was still in that shed tucked into the rugged rocks and I knew I had to get back to Barbados to see for meself.

"It is Fate that brought our lives together, Edward. When I realized who you was, and knowing what business you are pursuing, well, I just had to make this all known to you. It would be a way for me to make amends to your family, if you allow me to share the contents of the case."

"Family?" Edward said just above a whisper, looking hard at Pell. "As you know, I have no family. I have no desire to return to the land where I was born. And I have no reason to claim property that my 'father' stole for sport. Now that you have made your case, here is mine: I have no need for this lineage. I had no use for it as a boy, which is why I left Barbados. And I certainly have no use for it now, here in Carolina. Do not breathe a word of your story to anyone, Pell. It is of no use to me. You will have to find passage back to Barbados through some other means of blackmail."

"Blackmail?" Pell feigned hurt, holding his hand to his heart. "Why Edward, the thought had not even crossed my mind. I truly want to right a wrong from many years ago. I am reformed, and only want a part of the case's contents for my pension. Truth be told, I don't suspect old man Jenkins would even believe a word I say … though he might question his daughter's judgment in wanting to see you if he did know."

Edward lurched across the table at Pell, grabbing him by his shoulders and lifting him out of his chair and into the table's edge. "Now you listen, Pell," he whispered, "I will not be threatened or blackmailed. You have told your tale. Now keep it to yourself. I would sooner kill you than pay you off or take you aboard my ship for such a passage. Take a good look at my eyes, and know that I am telling the truth!"

Edward pushed Pell back down in his chair, nearly tumbling him into a table behind him. He stood up, threw a coin on the table for his ale, and strode out the door and into the blinding light of day. He did not lessen his pace until he reached the waterfront, where he paced for several blocks. There was only one person he would rely on to tell him how to handle this matter. He made his way back to the livery, found his wagon and horse and raced to Brunswick.

Chapter Eight

The Reverend Eubanks was hunched over his table, charting species of fish in his well-worn leather-bound journal with the assistance of a magnifying glass. Years had been kind to him, with the exception of his eyesight that now threatened to vanish. He had been offered the opportunity to return to the kinder climate of the Caribbean on several occasions, or even back to his homeland England; but felt his ministry was here in the colony, and he was determined to live his days along the banks of the Cape Fear River even though he no longer stood in the pulpit regularly. Indeed, he had found another pastoral pursuit: river fishing, he discovered, was quite different from the surf fishing as he did back on the island. He was more successful at it, and the variety of his catches was plentiful. He often would take one or two younger members of his flock on his fishing jaunts, each one taking turns rowing along the marshy tidewaters of the Cape Fear. This brackish water was home to dolphin, manta rays, spots, bluefish, croakers and a host of pan fish, shrimp and blue crabs, perfect for an evening meal. It would be a rare day that Reverend would not catch enough for his dinner and for that of a member of the parish. Feeding fish to his charges, and teaching others to fish. That, he felt sure, was the ministry that he would pursue for the rest of his days. In the meantime, the Reverend cataloged his catches noting the best fishing spots on charts and thanked the Lord for this bounty.

While his replacement the honorable Reverend Locklear tended to the weekly sermons for Brunswick's congregation, it was Eubanks they preferred to have minister to their personal needs. His steady presence during the town's earlier years made him a fixture in the community, and that status would not likely be inherited by his successor.

Edward's knock on the door broke the Reverend's concentration.

"My word, it is late, son. Please come in, and I will see about fixing us something warm," he embraced Edward and ushered him inside. When he got close enough to see Edward's worry, he urged him to sit. "Edward, what is troubling you?"

"Oh, Reverend, the past has come to haunt me!" Edward told him of his meeting in the tavern with Pell. Burying his head in his hands, he exclaimed, "I have come so far from that place. This man threatens to ruin what I have been building all these years. What am I to do?" He looked up, and stared blankly at the merry fire in the stone fireplace. How many meals had he cooked on that hearth? This was his home as much as any place, and this man was his father more than any man could have ever been.

"That is quite a dilemma, Edward. If you take this ... his name is Pell, you say? If you take Pell up on his offer of a passage to Barbados in exchange for ill-gotten booty, you will be rid of him and have a tidy sum to start a life of your choosing with Lady Sarah in any port of call. But you also risk losing Sarah if you make such a deal because you will be admitting to your less-than-honorable lineage if you take possession of such booty," he said thoughtfully. "But, of course, you also risk losing her if Pell tells his story to most anyone in town. If it comes to that, your reputation will be compromised, to be sure." Reverend walked to the fireplace, and filled his white clay pipe with tobacco. Tamping it down with his thumb, the Reverend rooted around in the tinderbox for a small twig with which to light his pipe. After a long draw, and a satisfying exhale, he looked squarely at Edward.

"Go tell her yourself first."

Edward looked at him in disbelief.

"My boy, you have built your life on honestly and hard work. She knows you to be an honest man, and if you do not tell her directly, you risk the worst kind of retribution: a woman's scorn. If she has feelings for you as I see you have for her, she will hear you out. The truth will set you free. If you choose not to tell her and she hears of this tale from Pell or from anyone else--say her father--you are no better than the scoundrel your father was for his lie of a life when he left his wife and family in Bridgetown."

Silence hung in the air like tavern smoke.

"Family? Did I hear you right?"

Reverend Eubanks nodded. "Two brothers."

"Why have you not told me there were others? All these years, you have known, and you have not said a word." In an instant, Edward felt betrayed at the revelation that he had siblings.

"I did not tell you, Edward, because you had no right to claim them as your brothers. The few times that I tried to persuade Mistress Bonnet to meet you, she refused me. She said there was to be no connection between you and her two sons. Why, it was she who sponsored in part your passage to the colonies. I mulled it over many nights, whether to tell you, but it just never seemed the right thing to do. Now, however, it seems appropriate to be honest with you, as I urge to you be with Lady Sarah."

"I have two brothers. When I was younger, I wondered if I had brothers."

"Perhaps you would not have left Barbados had you known of them?"

"I…I would have tried to meet them, and be one of them. But they would not have had me, would they?"

"No," the Reverend smiled at Edward's sad realization. "No, I fear they would not. That is why I felt it necessary to shelter you. You already carried the weight of the world on your young shoulders when we were in Bridgetown, and I felt that a fresh start without looking back and without strings to a past you could never claim would be best for all. I hope you understand my reasoning, Edward."

Though it pained him to say it, Edward agreed that he understood why the family secret was kept all these years. To have family, even half-brothers, meant that he was not truly alone in the world as he always believed he was. He had at least a chance of claiming kinship, a strong pull to a lonely boy. But as a grown man with the future ahead of him, would it be right for him to try to introduce himself to his brothers? Did they even know of his existence? And would they feel threatened by his returning? Edward's head throbbed.

CHAPTER NINE

Though still undecided of how, or even if, to tell Sarah, Edward focused on his most immediate concerns: securing a ticket to the Winslow's Christmas Ball and finding proper clothing. Sandwiched between working on the ship Virginia for Mr. William Leslie that was due for completion in just a few weeks and overseeing the harvesting of King Moore's southern-most acres of timber, Edward had very little time to achieve his goal.

While he had neither the extra money nor time to have a proper suit made prior to the Ball, he felt sure he must attend. He tried to stuff thoughts of Barbados and Ignatius Pell to a dark corner of his mind, and concentrate on the brightness that Sarah could bring to his life as he made his way to Orton Plantation.

As Moore's plantation wealth grew, so did his house. From its small quarters that now hosted the overseer and his family of three, the plantation manor had grown with expansions on either side of the center two-story building. These side wings offered extra space for Moore's growing family on one side, and his enterprises on the other. From his book-lined study over-looking the river, King could watch his businesses grow. During the warm seasons, rice and indigo took center stage. In the fall, it was the liquid gold of pine sap and pitch, and in the winter, timber harvested and cured on his property awaited a buyer. King considered other ventures based on the needs of fellow colonists but for now, he contented himself with his current exports.

On this cold morning, King greeted Edward as he approached. One of King's servants had just lit a fire in the study and King was warming his hands and his backside, alternately.

"I do declare, Edward, you chose a raw day to come to call. I was not expecting you until the end of the week. Is there a problem in Wilmington?" His tone was mildly alarmed.

"Nothing to do with business, Sir," Edward was quick to reassure him. "This is somewhat of a social call, if you like."

"Oh, then sit down Edward. Here, take this chair and pull it to the fire. These cold mornings are working their way into my bones, I fear. I am too old to be so cold." Moore pulled up a second chair for himself as he motioned for Edward to sit in a straight back chair in front of the fire. Moore placed his chair even closer still and stuck his feet nearly into the crackling fire.

"Now, tell me, what brings you here today?"

"I have come to ask a favor, well, actually two favors, if possible. I have only yesterday learned of a ball in

Wilmington that…uh…the Jenkins' will be attending, and I feel it imperative that I be there to ensure that your business interests are furthered. I have neither an invitation nor a proper suit of clothing to wear, so I've come to you in hopes that you could secure both for me."

"My business interests?" Moore laughed heartily at Edward's approach, and Edward smiled sheepishly at being so transparent. "I suspect that you have your own tender interests in mind as much as my business interests. I have seen this interest of yours, and I would agree that you would be wise to attend this affair for your own interests as well as mine—it is at the Winslow plantation, is it not? I agree though you will need another coat. Have you a clean shirt?"

"Sir, what I have is clean, but I fear not proper. What am I to do?" deplored Edward.

"Fear not. There is time for proper attire to be made for you. I will call Bessie to take your measurements before you leave here today, and she will have a suit worth wearing before the night of the event. You will ride to Wilmington with the Mrs. and me, and we shall call on the Jenkins *en force*, so that you can offer Miss Sarah Jenkins a proper coach ride to the Ball. I suspect you might have guessed that we would also have an invitation?" Moore raised an eyebrow, quizzing Edward.

Immediately relieved, Edward relaxed for the first time that day. Closing their meeting with thankfulness for Moore's generosity, Edward promised to be at Orton Plantation in plenty of time for the carriage ride to the

Ball. He bid Moore farewell after offering a report of the month's business activities, and sought out Bessie around the back of the main house.

Riding his gray mare to and from the plantation gave him time to plan how he would broach the subject of his lineage with Sarah. He imagined both the worst and the best scenario, and felt compelled to pray for guidance.

"Dear heavenly Father, forgive me for not turning to you sooner. I have a heavy heart on this matter, and I am not sure how to start. I know you are wiser still than any man I could even hope to be, so I pray that you will offer me guidance. Direct me, Lord, on how to speak my fears to Sarah. If it is your will that I lose her, help me to accept that which I cannot change."

Before the day was out, he found Elijah, and asked that he deliver to Sarah a short note asking her to accompany him to the Winslow's gala. Elijah would leave in the morning, and Sarah would have her answer within her five-day request.

Relieved, Edward turned his full attention to the *Virginia*. Her topping out would require rigging the sails and putting the final touches on her nameplate. Each day was filled with labor-intensive steps of outfitting to prepare her for her launch just two days before Christmas, and one day before the Winslow's Christmas Ball.

Everyone in the boatyard hoped for good weather and the festivities that go with any boat launching. Tradition had it that upon completing a boat, the boatyard would host a festive launching, and the whole town would celebrate by bringing food and drink that would rival other grand feasts.

Just prior to launching, the *Virginia* would be christened. A tradition as old as civilization, christening a ship was meant to protect her from harm and peril. The tradition called for a bottle or jug of the best spirits her owner could afford. This bottle would be blessed, and then broken on a new ship's bow by a man who had the respect of the community. The bottle's contents would be poured by the owner onto the ship's deck and shared between the owner and high-ranking members of the town. The glass or goblet would then be tossed into the water, never to be used again.

In the case of the *Virginia*, the Reverend Eubanks was asked to offer a benediction, and then a bottle would be handed to King Moore, whose spirit of prosperity would embrace the ship for her owner, William Leslie, a long-time business associate of King's.

With this ceremony only a few weeks away, Matty was frantically trying to get the boathouse and yard in order, directing his crew to tidy their work areas as they were completing their tasks associated with the topping out. The *Virginia* was the ninth major ship to be built, and so her success was important to all who worked there.

A cold front brought snow to the region, a rarity as much as a nuisance; but after a few days, temperatures rose again to the usual fifty degrees of December, a blessing for the weeks that followed as the big day of commissioning approached.

That morning, Edward woke early and made biscuits for the feast that would take place directly after the christening. His role in the event was limited to helping cast the cradle-snug ship down a ramp of logs that were perfectly milled in rounds and laid side-by-side in a trough to the water. Using the slight incline of the shore's bluff to ease ships into the water, vessels rolled smoothly with little more than gentle guidance by the boatbuilding crew.

As he put his offering of biscuits on the long planked table just outside the boathouse, Edward noted that Matty wore his fatigue like a cloak, but his face showed signs of relief that everything was going along as planned.

Townspeople gathered on either side of boathouse's bluff-side doors that slide open to reveal the *Virginia*, and clapped at her presentation. Part of a well-practiced crew, Edward took his designated position on the port side of her cradle.

The Reverend Eubanks, Mr. William Leslie, and King Moore made their way to the head of the crowd at the doors, and each patted the hull's lower timbers for good luck. From a wooden box lined in purple cloth, Leslie presented a dark bottle of champagne to Moore. Before he took is place at the bow for the official commissioning, The Reverend Eubanks put his left hand on the bottle, and his right on the ship. He bowed his head. His makeshift congregation did the same.

"Dear heavenly Father, we are gathered here today on this auspicious occasion to bless this ship, the *Virginia* and commission her to service. We pray, oh Lord, that your hand is on this vessel all of her days, just as your hand is on each of us, your children. We pray, oh Lord, that this ship is safe upon the seas it travels, and that all who ride upon her sturdy decks will be free from trials and tribulations. Heavenly Father, may this ship carry with her your good graces to foreign lands, and may she find her way safely home to us one again, as your will allows.

"It is in your name that I present this vessel to service, Lord. Blessings on *Virginia*. Amen."

As the crowd murmured amen in response, they turned their eyes to Moore. He gave a practice swing with the bottle to the bow, judging his distance, and swung in earnest the bottle at the bow. Spray went everywhere, and the crowd cheered.

Upon Matty's signal, Edward and the other boatyard workers started pulling ropes that operated a giant network of pulleys which in turn set the *Virginia's* descent to the water in motion. Her cradle accompanied her for the short slide to the water until it met a set of blocks that separated it from the hull. Quickly, *Virginia* reached the water and floated on her own bottom, still tethered to shore with lines held taunt by the boatyard crew.

Again the crowd cheered, and Moore, Leslie, and the Reverend patted each other on the back and shook hands. As Edward and his co-workers pulled, coaxed, and secured the ship to the nearby wharf, townspeople flocked to food-laden tables.

On his way back up the bluff from the wharf, Edward noted that a few stragglers wandered through the boathouse. He stopped in his tracks when he recognized among them the wide-brim hat of Pell. For a split second, he considered fleeing the boatyard. But as Pell had come this far, Edward quickly determined that Pell was bound to seek him out.

Before he could act, Pell turned and faced Edward, raising his hand in greeting. Pell's gait quickly lessened the distance between them, and Edward stood motionless.

"Hello there, Edward. I say, this *is* a glorious day for the boatyard and the town, to be sure. I was hoping to run into you here." Pell seemed quite sure of himself, approaching Edward as if he were an old friend.

Edward grimaced. Looking around to see if anyone was nearby, he glowered at Pell.

"Why have you come, Pell?" Edward growled.

"There, there, Mate, I just came to see your ship be splashed. She does have lovely lines. I admire men who can actually craft such vessels out of wood … I have no such skills, a shame, I know." Pell looked toward the *Virginia* laying alongside the town's dock. "She is going to be a fast ship to keep up with, I can tell. She reminds me of a ship from the old days, but this is just an old man's folly, to talk of the old days, is it not, Edward?"

"I care not to hear anymore of the old days, Pell."

"Ah, then you have decided to take your chances on your future? I never thought of you as a gambling man,

Edward. But perhaps I am mistaken. Tsk, tsk," Pell shook his head mockingly.

"I come down from Wilmington to see the progress of your own ship. I thought perhaps you changed your mind about sailing for the islands, one in particular, and see the house where you was born, if you get me meaning. I come all this way on the back of a wagon that I stopped and asked for a ride, I did. I come to offer me services as navigator, as a friend. But if you think you will not want me services, I will be returning to Wilmington now. I suspect Mr. Jenkins will want to know my whereabouts this day."

Pell tipped his hat at Edward, and slowly turned toward the main road. Edward could see a buckboard wagon filled with revelers along the main road into Brunswick. Pell was hedging again.

Edward needed to stall him before he spoke with Jenkins.

"Pell, wait. I appreciate that you would come all this way for the launching of the *Virginia.* You and your friends should stay for a meal at least. Anyway, it is getting too late to travel back. You should stay, have your fill, rest. Jenkins will not miss you today, will he? I mean, you do not work for him every day, so he will not be looking for you. If you want to see my ship, I will show her to you.

"As for your offer to navigate, I have not yet decided her first destination. I have not secured charts or crew yet. I would not start that process of provisioning until I get closer to her commissioning, which will be summer." Edward hoped this would pacify Pell until he had time to decide what to do.

"Very good then. I hear tell this ship's owner is a very wealthy man. Perhaps he will overlook me shortcomings, and hire me on so that I can go to sea again. Have you any idea which way he is headed once he sets sail?"

"That is not information that I am privy to, but I can talk to King Moore. He knows Leslie well enough to ask. I could even ask King to put in a good word for you, if you like." Edward was at once repulsed and delighted at the thought of "helping" to get Pell as far away from Brunswick and Wilmington, and in particular, the Jenkins family.

"Well, that is mighty kind of you, Edward. If you want to help out an old sailor, I would be obliged. I must say, though, I would rather sail in your company to Barbados, but if I can get on another ship in that general direction, I can make it back to me retirement pension."

"I will speak to King before the week is out, and learn what I can about Leslie and his plans for the *Virginia*. When next I am in Wilmington, I will do what I can to arrange an introduction, or at the very least, try to get your name on the crew list. Pell, if I do this for you, will you be so kind as to keep what you know of my history to yourself?"

"Well, now, I could promise to do that if I am secured on a crew list for a ship heading south. If the good Mister Leslie has plans for taking her in the opposite direction, well, I am not sure there would be reason for me to go. I am getting on in years, and me joints, they do not like the cold so much anymore." Pell rubbed his elbow for effect.

Edward's face grew red. With much restraint, he said, "Pell, I will do as you ask. Now be honorable, and keep your thoughts to yourself. I have not determined what I am going to do. If you push me, though, my actions will be very clear. Do you understand me?" Edward's voice lowered to just above a whisper, as he leaned in closer to Pell.

"Aye, Edward. I get your meaning. I will say nothing for the moment. But keep this in mind: what I offer is more for you and less for me, so I cannot understand why it upsets you so. If the Lady Sarah is going to accept you for who you are, it will matter not what she learns from the likes of me. Now, may we go take a look at your ship?"

Edward nodded, then made a gesture in the direction of his home, just up the hill. The two made their way past the long table of food, taking a few biscuits and ham on their way.

Behind Edward's cottage was the rough-hewn shed that sufficed as a boat shed. Edward had carefully oriented it so that on the day of its commissioning, he could roll his ship to the water's edge on a series of logs unencumbered by fences or buildings. Once it reached the slight bluffs, the logs would ease it into the water. Edward knew he would have to build a series of moveable guides to help keep his ship upright and on the logs, but he had seen this done years earlier before the large cradle system was built at the boatyard. Sections of scaffolding would be slowly relocated to accommodate the ship on her trek to the water. Many hands were needed to guide a ship in this manner, but Edward knew this was the only way he could build his own ship. He could not afford to rent space in the boatyard, but he could use the facility's ingenuity to launch his own future.

When Pell saw the ship rising from the dirt and wooden base in the shed, he nodded his head in approval. "I see that her lines are similar to the *Virginia's*. That must be the signature look of the yard, is it not?"

Edward put his hand on the base of the transom, and looked up. The transom would carry a name befitting a ship of her class, but he often found himself at a loss for the right name.

"Yes, this flair here in the transom makes her a fast ship. She will be steady underway, as long as she has fair water under her keel. She is liable to rock quite a bit at anchor, though." Edward pointed out other attributes of his ship, explaining his design for the ship. She looked rather like a duck without her rigging but that would come later once she was near the water and away from the trees that lined the path to the water. Edward explained that the rigging would be slightly raked back for efficiency, and that he would carry tenders on deck fore and aft of the deckhouse. He said he would build these by the end of spring.

"When do you hope to launch, Edward?" Pell asked.

"Early summer. I am working on the booms and spars now, but it will take me until then to get them ready for rigging. One of the boatyard riggers said he would help me with rigging, so it will move quickly once I get her down to the river."

Pell seemed satisfied with that answer as he pushed his hat up, exposing his ruddy forehead. "Well, if you will keep me in mind for navigating her, I will keep me knowledge to meself until then. When you decide which way you is heading, you let me know. I can...well, let's just say I have access to charts and gear that will make our passage comfortable and swift," Pell offered genuinely.

Relieved that Pell would hold his tongue, Edward gave an audible sigh. That would give him time to tell Sarah himself. Or not. He would have to decide soon.

Upon completing their tour, Edward and Pell strolled back to the boatyard. Pell said he hoped to get more to eat if it had not yet been taken up, and then he and his friends were going to make their way back to Wilmington.

Edward saw Pell off and headed back to the boatyard, though he did not feel much like celebrating anymore. He joined Eubanks at the long table where he was helping himself to a pile of potatoes. The day was growing colder, and Edward turned his collar up and reached for a plate.

"That fellow you were talking to … is that someone you know from Wilmington, Edward?" Eubanks offered.

"Yes. That is Ignatius Pell. I was surprised he came today, but I think he is pushing me for a commitment to head to the islands. Reverend, I know not what to do."

"Indecision *is* a decision, my son. You must make a plan for yourself, and figure out all the consequences of disclosing your past," Eubanks said between mouthfuls of whipped potatoes. "Whichever choice you make, God will be with you. Pray, and He will show you what to do."

"The Winslow's Christmas Ball is tomorrow night, and I am riding with King and Mrs. Moore. I pray I will know what to do when I see Sarah," Edward half-heartedly said, as he bit into an apple dumpling.

"You will know, my son, you will know," comforted Eubanks.

Chapter Ten

Edward got an early start the day of the Winslow's party. Before heading to Orton, he stopped by Eubanks' cottage for breakfast.

"Ah, Edward, you are excited about this party, I see it in your eyes," said Eubanks as he opened the door for his friend.

"Nervous is more like it," Edward responded.

"I am sure it will all go well, son. And to mark this occasion as the festive event that it is, I want to give you something." Holding up his hand signaling Edward to wait, Eubanks disappeared into his bedroom and reemerged with a small package wrapped in muslin. He handed the package to Edward, and turned to prepare breakfast.

"What is this?" Edward gingerly held the package.

"Open it. I had it made for you for Christmas, but I think it will be a nice touch to your outfit this evening."

Carefully opening the package, Edward saw a soft, deep green vest trimmed in black and lined with dark blue velvet. There was a three-inch pocket on the inside secured by a neat row of small buttons hidden in a folded seam, the perfect place for important papers or money. On the outside, gold-colored round buttons shone brightly, and there was a small watch pocket on the left side. On the back was a sash clasped with a buckle, an added touch which would help the vest fit snuggly under an overcoat.

"This is magnificent! I've never owned something so lovely. Thank you for this, I'll wear it tonight." Edward said, overwhelmed.

"You are so welcome, Edward. I felt you needed something special in your wardrobe. All fine gentlemen must have proper attire. Mrs. Kelly is quite handy with a needle and thread, don't you agree?"

"Yes, yes! I would say so. I am thrilled to display her handiwork. This pocket will have to go empty, tonight, though." Edward peered into the velvet-lined pocket as he buttoned up the vest.

"Or, you could have this." Eubanks pulled a red gingham cloth sack from his own pocket, and handed it to Edward. "Happy Christmas, son. I have been saving this for a number of years, and it seems fitting to give it to you tonight. My father gave it to me when I was about your age, before I went into the ministry. I am giving it to you in honor of him. He would have liked you very much I am sure, and, as you have been like a son to me all these years, it seems appropriate."

Edward slowly took the sack and opened it. Inside was a gold pocket watch attached to a sturdy chain. The worn outer case was engraved with the letter "E".

"Eubanks, Edward ... it's about the same," explained Eubanks with a smile to Edward's unanswered question, as he helped Edward fasten the end of the chain to the vest's middle button.

Speechless, Edward hugged Eubanks in thanks. The two admired the vest and the watch, and then Edward helped get breakfast on the table after carefully removing his vest and watch to save them from soiling.

"You have a long day ahead of you, Edward," Eubanks said over coffee. Are you all planning on returning this evening?"

"No, the Moores have invited me to stay with them in their townhouse. We will be back tomorrow sometime."

"Very well. I had hoped that would be the case." Eubanks rose from the table and headed into his pantry. "You must show Mrs. Moore your gratitude for her hospitality. Take this with you." He handed Edward a bottle wrapped in linen. "It's a bottle of wine, and as I have no use for it, you might as well take it."

Edward thanked him for seeing after all the details that would make his time more enjoyable. Once he cleaned up the dishes, he said goodbye and headed back to his cottage to pack a small bag and to dress in his best shirt and pants.

Once he arrived at Moore's plantation, he was fitted in his new suit that Bessie made for him. She had some last minute alterations to the jacket, as she had not accounted for Edward's new vest. She surprised him with a pair of trousers, too, and though they were a little big in the waist, Bessie was able to quickly adjust the waistband to better fit Edward.

"I guess at you size, and I guessed pretty good, eh?" Bessie looked at her handiwork with pride.

"Bessie, you are a queen, in my opinion," said Edward. "Thank you for doing this fine work on such short notice."

Bessie was grateful for the acknowledgement, and beamed as she fussed over a few last stitches in the coat. "My, you sure look fine, Mister Edward. I bet you get all the ladies, tonight," she chuckled. "Or at de least, one," she winked.

Edward blushed at the thought that his interests were known to everyone at Orton, but that was to be expected in such a small community.

Once Edward's fitting was over, Edward changed back into his traveling clothes. Then he joined the Moores and Bessie in a waiting carriage for a trip that would take them the better part of the day. Traveling to Wilmington would include road travel along the King's Highway, two flat-board barge ferries across creeks, and then through the sandy streets of Wilmington to the north side where Winslow's plantation sat on the Cape Fear. Mrs. Moore wanted to stop at her townhouse to rest after the journey and to have a proper bath before dressing for the party, so an additional few hours were necessary for the trip that would have taken a few hours for Edward to make on horseback alone.

Passing the travel time with family stories, the Moores invited Edward to share the coming holidays with them. One of their sons, William, was coming of age this winter. He would soon take his place beside his father in running Orton, so it was important that Edward and he get to know each other well, Moore suggested.

Edward knew William, of course, and the thought of working directly under him did not entirely please him. For one thing, William was younger than Edward. For another, William had a lot to learn about running a plantation, and Edward was not too sure about how he would fare in his role as agent to the Moores under William's direction. But Edward reasoned to himself that the situation might be different in a few years when William took over the plantation's daily operations.

Unsure of when it would be proper to offer his hostess gift to Mrs. Moore, Edward took a chance and presented it to her as soon as the party arrived at the townhouse. "Mrs. Moore, this is for you, for being gracious enough to have me as a guest in your home this evening. I hope it meets your approval," Edward pulled the wine bottle from his case as one of the Moore's house servants unloaded it from the carriage.

"Oh, Edward, you are a thoughtful young man. Thank you. We will have a glass before we go to the party this evening," she said, eyeing her husband, "and NOT until then." She turned on her heel, lifted her skirts to keep them out of the sand and headed up the wooden stairs into the townhouse.

Edward thought it an odd name for a structure that rivaled any in Brunswick, but because it was her home away from the plantation, and it just happened to be in town, Mrs. Moore insisted all during the ride that it was a townhouse.

After resting, bathing, and dressing with Bessie's help, Mrs. Moore announced that she was ready to go to the ball. She looked stunning in her dark red ball gown and matching cloak (that Bessie most likely had made for her, Edward thought), and his appreciative nod did not go unnoticed.

"You are a vision of loveliness, my dear," called King, has he pulled on his coat to his tuxedo. "Confounded buttons. This jacket fit me last year, and now look at it. Bessie, can you help me with this?" King tugged at his waistcoat as Bessie ran to his side.

"Well I declare, Master, I do think it shrunk. Here, let me have dat, and I will see what I can do." She helped him take it off and carried it into an adjoining sitting room. Mrs. Moore looked annoyed at the delay, but took the opportunity to primp some more in the hall mirror, adjusting her hat and cloak.

"We are going to be late if Bessie has to alter that coat. I told you to have her fit it last week, Roger, and now you are asking her to do it? Humph." Clearly, she was unhappy.

"Now it will only be a minute, dear. Calm down." Then, turning to Edward, "see what a fine job she did for Edward in short order? She is a miracle worker, that Bessie is. Edward, that is a fine vest you have one. Did Bessie make that for you too?"

No, Mrs. Kelly of Brunswick made it for me. Reverend Eubanks gave it to me this morning as a Christmas gift, and he gave me this, too." Edward proudly pulled out his pocket watch.

King took a step forward and admired the watch, and fingered Edward's vest. "Both very fine gifts. What will you give to him in return?"

"I have no idea; I haven't had time to think about it." Edward cocked his head thoughtfully.

Just then, Bessie reentered the room with King's jacket. She helped him into it, and he fastened his buttons with ease.

"See? I told you Bessie was a miracle worker. Just look at this coat now. It fits like it should. Thank you, Bessie, for repairing it."

"Oh, I didn't do no repairing. I figured you might be needing a slightly larger coat this year, so I added a few inches to the measurements of last year's coat, and made it de same time I was making one for Edward. See how it fit you? I even added a special pocket for you right here on de inside for your snuff," Bessie added. Then realizing she'd let King's little secret out in front of Mrs. Moore, she excused herself from the room hurriedly.

"Oh, never mind that, let's just go," said King, and he ushered a startled Mrs. Moore out of the door, with Edward following close behind carrying his and King's hats. Edward listened to the two of them bicker over King's snuff habit for a few streets until the carriage reached the Jenkins' home. Their driver, Bessie's man Shelton, hopped down from atop the carriage and knocked on the Jenkins' door to announce their arrival.

Shortly, Mr. and Mrs. Jenkins and Sarah appeared at the door, and Edward and King stepped out of the carriage to offer greetings and to help them get in. Edward took one look at Sarah, and he knew he had to tell her his story tonight. Surrounded by a cloak of black trimmed in emerald green, she was radiant. Sarah and Edward had not spoken or seen each other for several weeks, so their excitement in seeing each other was surely noticeable to everyone in the carriage.

That evening's ball was the event of Wilmington. Carriages of every description lined the entryway to the Winslow's manor house, a stark white two-story structure with a wide porch facing the expansive lawn to the rear of the house, and an even wider porch lined with chairs and tables facing the river.

Guests mingling on either porch were protected from December's winds by a series of canvas cloths hung from the ceiling and secured on the edge of the porch, and warmed by a portable raised fireplace that had a metal chimney. King and Thaddeus nodded hellos and shook hands with several of the men standing on the porch, knowing that they too would find solace out here and room to partake of certain habits, snuff notwithstanding.

But the main attractions were inside. Skirted tables laden with food, drink, and massive floral arrangements lined one side of a makeshift ballroom, and on the other side were tables and chairs. Rousing music greeted guests as they entered the room, and Edward saw couples twirling around a hall, flashes of color revolving in grand sweeps. In an instant, he realized with horror that he had no idea what to do, or how to dance. This was the first time he'd ever been to a ball! His first thought was to flee but when he turned around, he saw Sarah who was being helped out of her cloak, and her beauty halted him in his tracks. Her dress was the same deep green as her cloak's trim, and her hair was done up with small clumps of holly and baby's breath. Long sleeves were trimmed in ivory lace, as was the plunging neckline. In that instant, Edward felt his heart jump to his throat. He could not speak. He could not move.

For what seemed an eternity he looked at Sarah without any sense to propriety. Sarah extended her hand and he took it, and following King's generous example just ahead of him, wrapped her hand through his extended arm. Edward led her to a quiet place where he hoped to tell her how lovely she looked, and how inadequate he felt, given his two left feet.

"Sarah, you are by far the loveliest here this evening," Edward started, but stopped when he saw Sarah blush. "I hope you will forgive me, but I must tell you that I do not know how to dance. It is embarrassing to admit but I have never been to this kind of affair before."

Sarah patted his hand and smiled. "Edward, dancing is not the only reason I've come tonight. Certainly, we can enjoy the evening together without dancing?"

Pleased with her response, Edward offered to get her a plate of food. But making his way back through a growing crowd, he saw Sarah talking with another man. Instantly hot with jealousy, he counted to five before approaching. "Here you are, Sarah, I think there is a table available over there," he nodded at the far end of the room, hoping Sarah would get the message, or that the man would.

"Oh, yes, Edward, that would be fine. Patrick Monahan, this is Edward Marshall, the gentleman I was telling you about," Sarah said, making introductions. Edward curtly said hello.

"Miss Sarah tells me you are a shipbuilder, Mr. Marshall. I have a desire for a fast trading ship. Perhaps we can talk in a bit about it."

Edward was somewhat relieved. "Yes, I build ships with a boatyard in Brunswick. The person you really should speak with is not here this evening, but I can certainly tell him about your ideas."

"Oh, I misunderstood. I thought Sarah told me you were building your own ship."

Edward paused. "Yes, I am, but it is for my own use. I've neither the space nor the equipment to build ships for others at this time. You would be better served to deal directly with the boatyard. I am curious, Mr. Monahan, why you would not consider one of the fine shipbuilders here in Wilmington. There are several on the waterfront, and their operations are far bigger than what we have to offer in Brunswick."

"Cost. Many of these builders here charge for the space they occupy, and smaller builders, like you for instance, don't have the overhead. I am a businessman, so my loyalties are to my purse strings," he said with a smile and a wink in Sarah's general direction.

Noting Edward's face was starting to redden, Sarah graciously asked to be excused from business talk and headed through the crowd toward a vacant table.

"I see. Well, if keeping costs to a minimum is critical to you, then you should speak directly with Matty Trumbell, the owner of the boatyard. I am sure he will be able to give you a fair deal. The building is located on the riverfront, so the next time you are in town, just stop by and introduce yourself." Edward wanted to join Sarah as quickly as he could, but Mr. Monahan had other ideas.

"I detect that you are interested in Miss Sarah."

"She accompanied me to this ball, yes."

"I see. Well, if it is acceptable to you, I would like to dance with her. She is a fine dance partner, and if her dance card is not full with your signature, I would like to sign it next."

Dance card? Edward knew nothing of this custom, so he nodded, excused himself, making his way to Sarah's table. As he approached, he noticed that she indeed had taken a small card from her purse, and laid it on the table beside her plate.

"Sarah, is that your dance card?"

"Yes, Edward. I thought if you wanted to, you could sign it first. That way, you get my first dance, and no other man can cut in front of you. And, since you don't dance…well, it is a socially accepted device to keep others at bay, so we have a chance to enjoy the music together."

"I appreciate your thoughtfulness, but Mr. Monahan tells me you are a good dance partner. I don't want to deprive you of fun, if you prefer to dance."

"Edward, if I feel like dancing, I will. For now, I would like to enjoy your company here. Please tell me, how was the launching of the *Virginia*? And how is your boat progressing? It's been awhile since we've talked, so we have some catching up to do."

Edward smiled at having a chance to tell her about the launching, and about other matters closer to his heart. He wasn't sure how to start, so he started with the *Virginia's* launching. "It was a successful day for the boatyard, and everyone in town turned out for it. Quite a few visitors from out of town also came to see it. One of them, I think you know."

"Oh?" Sarah asked.

"Ignatius Pell came to see the launch, and to check on the progress of my own ship." Edward watched as Sarah's eyebrows rose. She gave no recognition of knowing any of what Edward was about to tell her.

"The man who works for my father? I suppose he would have an interest in ships. I gather that he has spent some time aboard in years past."

"He has indeed. His past and mine well, Sarah, they are intertwined. It is complicated, and I really am not sure where to begin but I know I have to tell you. Before I start, please let me say that what was in the past was in the past. And you, Sarah, I believe to be my future, so please hear me out before you say anything."

Sarah put down her fork, dotted her mouth with a cloth napkin, and put her hands in her lap. Edward took a deep breath before he spoke.

"Sarah, Ignatius once worked for my father, who commanded his own ship. Ignatius was a crew member who was very close to him as his boatswain … similar to a plantation foreman. And in this capacity, he learned a great deal about my…my parents. He has approached me on numerous occasions, and has offered to help navigate my ship to an island where he first met my father. When I suggested that I did not want to return there, he threatened to come directly to you to tell you about my parents. I felt it was time for me to tell you myself, rather than risk you hearing it from the likes of him."

"Edward, you've not spoken of your homeland or your parents to me before. What could possibly be so terrible that Ignatius would hold that over on you?" Sarah bit her tongue, for she had not intended to speak before he was done.

Flustered, Edward blurted, "My father was a pirate and my mother was…my mother was a woman of ill repute."

Sarah's hand flew to her mouth. "This can't be!"

"Ignatius is telling the truth, Sarah. He told me enough to make me see that there cannot be coincidence. I grew up in an orphanage and with Reverend Jonathan Eubanks, who brought me to this coast. And while my background is not ideal, I can assure you that I have made myself into as honorable a gentleman as possible." Edward registered the shock on Sarah's face. "I am not a man of great means, or even graces like your friend Mr. Monahan. I can't offer you a fancy home, and I don't even own the suit I am wearing except for this vest, which was given to me this morning by the Reverend. I have but a few possessions, Sarah, but I would offer them all up gladly if you would become my wife and sail with me upon my ship."

Sarah looked directly into his eyes. But before she could speak, Patrick Monahan breezed up to the table and asked Edward if he could steal Sarah away for a dance.

"No!" Edward nearly shouted.

"Yes," Sarah calmly stated.

Edward's face fell as Sarah rose to meet Monahan's hands. She walked slowly, deliberately allowing Monahan to guide her into the waves of swirling couples on the dance floor. He watched after them for a few minutes, until he realized his hand was in a fist and his shirt collar felt as if it were two sizes too small. He shot out of his chair and stormed out of the manor by way of the smoky haze on the back porch that was filled with men escaping for a quick smoke and a snort. His pace quickened when he saw Thaddeus Jenkins, who hailed Edward as he hurried past.

Not knowing any other place in town, he headed to the tavern where he once shared a drink with Pell. He soon found himself in front of the place, and hesitated only a moment before entering. Immediately, the smell of malt and human stink slapped him in the face as he pushed the heavy door open. Laughter and rough voices rose like the color on his face, and within a few minutes, he had found an empty chair and a full glass. And Pell.

"You told her, didn't you?" Pell seemed almost pleased at Edward's appearance. "She rejected you. Now that tells you a bit about the lass. It's better to know this sort of thing now, me boy. It gets it out of the way."

Edward lunged at Pell and shoved him up against the wall. "This is your fault, Pell. If you hadn't threatened to tell her, I never would have, and she and I would be planning a future together!"

"If'n she would have you," Pell squeaked out. "Don't you see, Edward? She reacted to your lineage, not to the telling. It would be the same years from now when you finally felt the guilt pushing you to tell her what's on your heart. And then what? You would have brought her into a life with you based on a lie that you is something you ain't, and that ain't respectable. At least this way, you've acted honorable, you told her the truth. She can't fault you for that."

Edward gave him a final shove and collapsed into his chair, knowing that Pell was right. For all of his shortcomings, Pell was capable of seeing the truth, even though he delighted in telling it to add to another's misfortune.

That night, Pell took him to his quarters and did his best to make his new best friend comfortable. In the morning, Pell assured him, he would see to it that Edward returned home so they could start planning their voyage.

CHAPTER ELEVEN

When he described Sarah's reaction to Eubanks a few days after the incident, Eubanks was sympathetic, but not surprised.

"Give her time, Edward. I do not know her well, but perhaps she will come around when she realizes that you were speaking honestly."

"I don't think she will care, at this point. That fellow Monahan was right there to offer her comfort, and he is a proper suitor. I am not. It would be in her best interests to accept him as a suitor. But I can't help but wonder if that is really the kind of life she wants. She had said numerous times that her desire was to see the world. I don't suppose that Monahan would deprive her of that."

In the months that followed the ruinous ball, Pell scurried about Wilmington collecting gear and charts and crew. It didn't take Jenkins long to spread the word among his friends in Wilmington and surrounding regions once he learned the truth, and so there was little hope of future work for Edward. And as he did not want to hurt Matty's business in any way, Edward resigned from the boatyard.

While he missed his friends there, he now had the freedom to work full time on his ship. He used his stash of savings to finish and outfit it. Edward asked Mrs. Kelly to sew sails, and helped her with measurements based on similar designs he'd seen in Matty's boatyard. Edward's friends Richard and Elijah helped out whenever they could, and even Matty offered a hand when it came time to build a moveable scaffold-like cradle to move the ship toward the river's edge.

By the end of April, the boat was nearly ready for topping out. Together with a few true friends and boatyard workers looking to earn some money on the side, Edward guided his ship to the water on the laid logs. Through the town's streets it paraded, and a small crowd followed the curious procession and watched the ship as it descended the slight bluff.

Unlike the *Virginia*, Edward's ship did not have the benefit of a full day commissioning celebration. But just before the launch, the Reverend made his best effort to bless this ship and all who sailed her, and then pour libations over her deck and into the river. A few people brought food and spirits, but news of Edward's past had hardened many of the townspeople's hearts against Edward. Even King had declined any further services offered by Edward, so Edward pressed on toward his departure date. It seems that King and Thaddeus Jenkins' long-time relationship counted more with King than did Edward's earnest efforts to make his own way in the world.

But Jenkins had another incentive to shut Edward out of the loop as broker between King and himself. He wanted Edward to stay away from his daughter. "She was not brought up to fall for the likes of him," he fumed at Isabel as she comforted her daughter one evening. "Mr. Monahan has more salt in his entire body than that Edward has in his table's salt dish, and I'll be damned if Sarah is ever going to see him again."

"Dear, you are overreacting. Can't you see that Sarah is upset?" Isabel did her best to calm him down.

"Upset? I am upset that he tried to hoodwink her. He almost had her snared; but now he's the one who's upset, I dare say. Sarah you are not to see him again, do you understand me?"

"Yes, Father, I hear you," Sarah sobbed. "Now please leave me alone."

"I will leave you alone when you agree to Mr. Monahan's generous offer of marriage. He is a fine, upstanding citizen of this community, and his wealth will see you in comfort for the rest of your days."

"Father, I do not want to marry Patrick. He is…oh, this is just too much to think about right now. Please let me rest."

"Yes, dear, we've all had a frightful few months. Can we please let this rest for a few weeks?" added Isabel, hoping to sooth her husband's temper.

"A few weeks? Alright, but no more. By the first of June, I want you to give Patrick an answer; In the affirmative, young lady. He is going to be your husband, so just get used to the idea." Jenkins slammed Sarah's bedroom door so hard that plaster fell from the walls.

Isabel continued to rock her daughter as if she were a child again, gently stroking her long hair.

"Sarah, darling, perhaps a change of scenery would do you good. Would you like to go to Annapolis with me? It's time for the annual races, and we've not been in several years. We could make a trip out of it and see our friends there."

Sarah sobbed, "anything, if it will keep me from having to marry Patrick."

"Well, you can't put it off forever, and your father thinks it would be good for you. But we can delay your answer for a little while if we prolong our stay," Isabel said wryly. "What do you say? Shall I start making plans?"

Sarah sat upright. "Yes. Let's have a change of scenery."

Isabel kissed Sarah's forehead, smoothed her hair back one last time, and walked toward the door. As soon as she was out of sight, Sarah flew to her writing desk and scratched a note to Edward explaining that she had been sequestered in her room all these months, but that she needed to see him. She wrote that she was heading to Annapolis, and maybe they could meet there if his ship was ready. Then she sealed her note and called Marna to her room.

"Marna, I need you to get this note to Edward just as quickly as you can. I don't know what else to do, but I must contact him at once. Father won't let me leave the house, and I…" she started to cry again.

"Miss Sarah, you know if I take dis for you, I can get in trouble," Marna shook her head. "But I see by de look in your face that I get in more trouble if I don't take it." Marna smiled as Sarah brightened a bit. "I like that boy, Edward. I like him so much more than that fat Patrick. You don't need to be with no fat boy, Miss Sarah. He eat you out of house and home. Besides, he is interested in money—and not much else. He work too hard chasing de dollars, and he won't spend too much time at home with you. That ain't no fun for you, Child. No, I much prefer de red head. They a lot of trouble, dem red heads, but dey is so much more fun," she winked as she hid the note in the folds of her red checkered skirt and headed out the door. Sarah was relieved, and started to pack for Annapolis.

CHAPTER TWELVE

Marna waited until morning to venture into town. She asked Isabel if she could visit a sick friend down near the waterfront, and Isabel agreed to let her go as long as she returned before noon. Carrying a sack of biscuits with Sarah's note tucked in the cloth, Marna hoped to find someone heading to Brunswick by ferry, the quickest way to go, given all the water separating the two towns. As she looked up and down the waterfront for someone to carry her message to Edward, she caught sight of a familiar face.

Elijah was heading her way on Edward's gray mare. They'd seen each other during the past year when Elijah and Edward stopped by the Jenkins' house to collect monies from Mr. Jenkins.

Marna always liked the looks of him.

"Mr. Elijah, how do?" she called out to get his attention. When he recognized her, he tipped his hat, dismounted and stood out of the way of a passing wagon, waiting for her to approach.

"Miss Marna, what brings you so far from the house this sunny day?"

"I got a package for a friend. And what brings you to dis town?"

"Mister Marshall wanted me to come and get some things. He sets sail in the morning, so this is the last chance I have to get things together. I think he wanted to come hisself, but he too busy getting things ready to go," Elijah leaned in closer to Marna. "Too busy and too sad, I think."

"My Missy, she sad too. You think we could make it so's they not sad?"

"Depends," said Elijah. "Depends on what her true colors is. Mr. Marshall, he's true blue, even though his father wasn't. But that don't make him a bad man. He's always been fair an' honest with me, and that counts a lot."

"Well, I think dat red-headed man is nice, too, much nicer than that old fat Patrick Monahan Mister Jenkins is partial to for my Missy."

"Ah, that is a bit concerning."

"I wonder, if you go back home tonight if you could take something--a little note--to you red-headed friend. It from my Missy."

"I can do that. Do you know what it say?"

"No, I don't read much. And it ain't none of my business anyway, it's between de two of them."

"Well, it will stay with the two of them, I can't read so well neither. But I can deliver it. Tell your Missy I will take it with me when I head home. Uh, do the biscuits I smell come with the delivery?" Elijah pointed at the sack.

"Yes, hep yourself." Marna looked pleased that she had delivered her message <u>and</u> had given Elijah a taste of her cooking. He was such a nice looking man, even if he was a bit older, she thought. "Are you going to be sailing with Mister Edward?" Marna coyly asked.

"No Ma'am, I am a shipbuilder, not a sailor. I will stay in Brunswick at the boatyard. They all really nice to me, and I respect them too. Besides, it's closer to Wilmington, and I sort of like it here." Elijah smiled and reached into the sack, lifting a covering cloth, and smelled the biscuits for effect.

"Thank you kindly, Miss Marna. I left so long ago this morning, I am hungry again."

Marna made a quick curtsy and watched as Elijah mounted the horse. He tipped his hat to her again, and rode off in the direction of the largest chandlery where he would purchase a few more spare blocks for the rigging. But just as she turned around to head back home, a large arm stopped her short.

"Passing notes along, are we now?"

It was Patrick Monahan.

"Not that it is any of you business, Sir. Now take your hand off of me."

"Who was that man?"

"Oh he ain't nobody."

"Well, if he ain't nobody, then how do you know him, and why did you give him a sack?"

"He just a friend, and he was hungry," Marna wrenched her arm away from Monahan, and started to walk away, but he stepped in front of her.

"I suspect your master would like to know what you are up to. Let's go visit him together." Monahan grabbed her elbow and firmly held it, directing her on to Jenkins' warehouse.

"My mistress know where I am, she said I could come out on my own." Marna was getting frightened. As a slave, she was subject to severe punishment if she was caught doing something she wasn't supposed to. She knew her mission would upset Jenkins, and she would be in trouble. By the time they got to the warehouse, Monahan's tightening grasp was hurting her. She tried to struggle free, but he only held her tighter.

"Mr. Jenkins, hello!" Monahan bellowed, waving frantically to catch Jenkins' attention above the din of the warehouse. When Jenkins saw him and Marna, he immediately grew alarmed and rushed to where they stood.

"What in heaven's name…? What is going on?"

"I came across Marna and Marshall's man on the road there, and she was handing him a sack. I was close enough to hear part of their conversation, and there was some talk about a note." Monahan was proud of his disclosure. "It seems Marna here fancies the 'red head', rather than…I believe you were referring to me, were you not, Marna?" He patted his bulging stomach for emphasis.

"I didn't mean nothing by it, honest." Marna was clearly scared, and she blurted out her story. "Mistress Isabel said I could come out, and I happened to run into Mister Elijah who was hungry. I give him a sack of biscuits. That's all."

"It was a kindly thing to do, Marna," Jenkins said calmly. "What's this about a note?"

"I in trouble either way," she sighed, barely audible.

"Excuse me, Marna?" Jenkins was growing impatient.

"Sir, I don't mean no disrespect, but if Missy Sarry give me something, that's what I done. I don't know what it said, I only know that she was mighty upset."

"Marna, thank you for telling me. When did Elijah say he was heading home?"

"Tonight after he go to the chandlery. That nice Mister Marshall is leaving in the morning, so I 'spect that Missy was just writing him a note to say goodbye."

"Very well, then, Marna. Thank you for telling me." Then, turning to Monahan, he said, "Mr. Monahan, thank you for bringing this to my attention, but I think this is a family matter."

"I thought you would want to know about it. If we are done here, I have work to attend to now. Good day." He tipped his hat to Jenkins, glared at Marna, and left.

Marna began to excuse herself as well, but Jenkins stopped her before she could go.

"Marna, you have been loyal to my family for many years. I hope that our conversation can be kept between us, now."

Marna nodded.

"Mr. Monahan comes from a good family. He is an honest man, and he would be a good provider for Miss Sarah. Isn't that what she deserves? To be well cared for?"

Again, Marna nodded.

"What you may not know, Marna, is that Mr. Marshall is the son of a pirate. His very name is a lie. His mother was a whore, and he has their blood in his veins. I have never met a man who did not carry with him his father's likeness in some way. From the very beginning, Mr. Marshall has presented himself to Sarah and to the rest of us as something he is not. He is not an honorable man, Marna. Now, you wouldn't want him to be dishonest with Sarah, would you?

Marna shook her head.

"Good. Now that we understand each other, please return to Sarah and tell her that you did as she asked."

Marna curtsied and nearly ran out of the warehouse and back up the hill to the Jenkins' home. When she got there, she breathlessly told Sarah what had happened.

"Missy, I don't know what you put in de note, but dat fat Mister Monahan sure is mad dat I passed it along."

"Oh, Marna, it's all going so terribly wrong! I have to see Edward before he leaves. I am sure he thinks I hate him, but I don't! I love him, and I don't want him to leave without knowing it. I want to go with him! Please help me see him again, Marna."

"Missy, I deliver de note. He will have it tonight, and then maybe he will stay and you can talk to him before…" she stopped talking when she realized Isabel had walked into the room.

"Before she marries? Marna, bring us some tea. I want to speak with Sarah alone." Isabel was firm with Marna, but her eyes were fixed on her daughter.

When Marna left the room, Isabel softly closed the door behind her.

"Sarah, your father is interested in your well being. I dare say he would have his only daughter traipsing about on a ship, even if it were with a man who <u>wasn't</u> the son of a pirate. That Mr. Monahan doesn't exactly suit you is of little consequence. You must keep your head about you and marry a man who will be able to provide for you."

"Is that what you did?"

"My choices were my own, dear."

"But you are not letting me have a choice at all, Mother."

Isabel sat down on the bed, and smoothed her skirts about her. She sat perfectly straight, and looked at Sarah. After a long silence, she stood up, and took a small bag from under the bed. She then pulled several items from one of the trunks that Sarah had started packing the night before, and stuffed them into the small bag.

"You will want to travel light this evening if you are to see Edward before he leaves. I will have Marna pack a meal, and she will chaperone you on the ferries to Brunswick and aboard with Edward. Do not talk about your destination to anyone you meet along the way. In the morning, I will leave for Annapolis as we planned, leaving just after your father goes to the warehouse. That will give you a week to visit with Edward and to be aboard his ship, for I think that is the only life he will ever be able to provide for you. I want him to bring you to Annapolis where you shall find me at the Crosby's home. I will make excuses for you that you are visiting other friends, but you must return to Wilmington with me. Then, if you still have a heart for Edward and his shipboard lifestyle, you will have to confront your father by yourself. This is the only time I will intervene on your behalf."

Sarah flew at her in a hug, and then dashed out of the room to help Marna with food for their trip.

Isabel sighed and continued to pack.

Meanwhile, Thaddeus Jenkins had a different tact in mind. He sent two of his men from the chandlery in search of Elijah. When they found him, they beat him and returned to Jenkins with the sack of half-eaten biscuits and the note.

CHAPTER THIRTEEN

Edward hunched over the worktable in the boatyard, paintbrush in hand. Mixing the colors to get a decent green was more of a challenge than he thought it would be, but he needed it to be perfect: this green was going to be the compliment to the gold lettering on the stern, the finishing touch to his ship. He had only one more task to complete her, and this was it.

Before the party at the Winslow's plantation, Edward had a notion to name his ship "Sarah". But he felt there was no reason to drag the memory of that disastrous day with him, so he spent several months searching his heart for the perfect name for his ship. While he came up with some good candidates, none seemed just right. One afternoon, while he fished in the marsh creeks nearby, he had an idea. He rowed over to the still creeks behind Smith Island, and hiked to the ocean side. After walking miles along the beach, Edward found the place that Pell had told him about, the place he avoided visiting until now.

Edward climbed the dune that overlooked the entrance to the Cape Fear River, where the island's sandy shoals whipped like a dragon's tail up to thirty miles off shore to snare unwary sailors. At the top of the dune, Edward saw a lone weather-gnarled tree, and his heart pounded. Softly, he approached the tree, as if it were hallowed ground. A carpet of orange and black sand daisies surrounded the tree's base. Edward fell to his knees and sobbed.

"Mother," he started softly, the sound of a word so infrequently spoken lingering. "Mother, if you can hear me…" Edward looked around to see that he was quite alone. "Mother, I have not come to visit this spot before, and I don't know when I shall return. I've come to pay my respects, and to tell you how I feel. I did not ask to be brought into this world but here I am, and I now bear what secret you and my father shared. It was not fair of you or right, but what is done is done. I think I can forgive you because you fell in love with him and you accepted him for what he was. I assume you forgave him. I don't know that I can do that. He turned his back on me, and I feel the sting doubly now that I am alone. My adopted town has turned its back on me because of him, because of who he was, and what he did."

"I hope to set myself apart from him and his deeds, Mother. I can never be free of my blood, but I can start a new life with what little he supposedly put aside for you. Pell is convinced it is still there. I suppose that was the most honorable thing my father did, was to put something aside for you. Something of value. As you gave me the gift of life, I will try to make the most of it, despite him."

Edward wiped his eyes, and took once last look at the spot, and the tree before he walked back to his rowboat. As he pulled toward the other side of the river, he decided on the name for his ship.

Months of long days saw the rigging rise, sails bent on, and lines mastered and coiled on deck. His crew of three, Ignatius Pell, Clarence Davenport, and a young lad eager to set sail by the name of Theodore "Jolly" Quince, were stowing their gear and rolling caskets of water and provisions on board.

Edward's small ship was fast, and with it, he had hoped to carry stores on contract. But since most everyone in Brunswick knew his heritage, he was unable to secure his first shipment to transport for a fee from this town.

Eager to reach Barbados, Pell convinced Edward that the voyage could be a swift passage if they did not load the ship too heavily anyway. The islands, he told Edward, would be the best stop so that they could get more money for future travels.

Edward had time to think about the treasure for a few months, and was pleased to go after it. That treasure held the promise of a new start, one that he could design, given enough wealth. And since he had no cargo, he had to get funds elsewhere. The treasure seemed as good a source as any.

That evening as he fixed supper in the galley of his ship, he looked over what few possessions he carried on board from his cottage. The table and benches were functional, and he modified his bedding for comfortable accommodations in the aft "captain's quarters". His galley gear was the same as what he'd used in his cottage kitchen, and he even built a small pantry-like cupboard for his personal stores, much like he'd had in his cottage. Reverend Eubanks offered to take on the chore of selling his cottage and holding the monies until Edward could return, knowing that it would be awhile before people in town forgot who had owned it. Though Edward had counted on this money for his travels, he agreed that a fast sale was not likely. Given his need for funding, he viewed what Pell often referred to as his "inheritance" differently now.

His crew had made their bunks as secure as possible in the forward cabins, with Pell taking over the largest of the crew's quarters as his navigation station. The three were using their last night ashore to say goodbye to family and friends, or, in Pell's case, to get more than one last good pint in before the voyage, which Edward swore would be a dry one.

As the evening wore on, Edward wondered about Elijah. "He should have been back by now," he thought. While it would have been nice to have the extra rigging blocks on hand before he set sail, he was more concerned about being able to say goodbye to his friend.

"Perhaps he needed to rest before returning," Edward said half aloud, "it can be a long journey."

He was jarred from his thoughts by a loud thumping on the hull, and a call of "ahoy". Coming on deck, he saw Eubanks standing on the dock. He had at his feet a box.

"Good evening, Edward, I thought we could share this evening with a bit of stew and a few other things I've found in my pantry," Eubanks called.

"Yes, yes! Come aboard. Here, let me help you." Edward scrambled down the boarding plank and deftly balanced the box that Eubanks brought. "Any sign of Elijah this evening, Reverend? I expected to see him earlier today."

"No, I have not seen him. Perhaps he stayed the night in town. Perhaps he doesn't like goodbyes anymore than I do."

"Well that I can understand. But I will be back soon. I will bring back news from Barbados, which my navigator tells me is not too far away."

"You have plans to seek out family there?"

"I might as well. I would like to know more of my family's history. They may not accept me, but I can accept them just the same. I want to at least try to make amends for my father's actions where I can."

"Son, you are not responsible for his misdeeds. You should focus on your own future."

"Yes, I know that, and I plan on it. But I want to revisit where I came from, so I can clear my mind of all that was in the past first."

"Are you sure that running away is a good idea, Edward?"

"I don't see it as running away but rather as moving forward. My future is not here, Reverend. I have no livelihood here. And since Sarah would have nothing to do with me, it makes little sense to stay here any longer."

Eubanks slowly opened the box Edward carried aboard for him, revealing salt meat and dry goods. There were also three Bibles. "Well, as long as you are going, I want you to take the Good Word with you. If you have the occasion, please share the Gospel with another who is in need of hearing it. Knowing that you might show someone the Light will make it easier for me to see you go."

"Thank you, Reverend. I will return some day, and we will keep in touch. Thank you for all the kindness you have shown me over the years. I will never forget." The two shared a meal and quiet conversation about old times that evening before saying their final goodbyes.

CHAPTER FOURTEEN

The dawn's low tide and slow winds gave Edward and his crew a few extra hours to secure all provisions in place aboard, and Pell a few extra hours to sleep off the previous night's tavern visit.

When the waters washed over the shoals and oyster beds just beyond the wharf, Edward called to his crew to hoist the forward sail and start untying the dock lines that held them fast. With these light breezes, he thought it would take awhile to get away. When the foresail finally filled with air, Clarence and Jolly made their way forward and released the bow lines so that the ship's bow started to angle out away from the dock. Moving aft, they untied the midship's lines. They would untie the aft lines last, using them to help pivot the ship away from the dock as her sail filled with air. Once the ship was away from the dock, they would then hoist the main and cutter sheets, and finally the mizzen on the aft deck which would help in steering the ship. Then, they would be on their way down river to the mouth of the Cape Fear, passing Smith Island on their portside, and into the Atlantic.

Before Clarence and Jolly could release the midship's lines, a woman's shout for help froze them in their tracks. Running toward them was a tired looking negress, her dress a mess. Just behind her was a buckboard wagon.

Edward immediately recognized Marna, and raced to the bow to fasten the forward lines. He ordered Clarence to grab the foresail, and make it fast, while Pell clamored topside to see what the commotion was. Jolly positioned the boarding plank when the ship was back alongside the dock, and Edward sprang to the dock, meeting Marna mid-stride.

"Marna, what are you doing here? I thought…" He looked up to see Sarah in the back of the approaching wagon cradling a wounded Elijah. When he reached the wagon, he gasped at the sight of Elijah's bloody head that rested against Sarah's chest.

"What happened? Elijah, what happened?"

"We found him near the ferry landing in Wilmington, Edward," Sarah spoke first. "Marna said she spoke with him yesterday in town, and…we were on our way to see you this morning and found him lying in the woods near the ferry. I didn't know what else to do, but this nice man came along and helped us get him in the wagon," she continued, nodding in the direction of the wagon driver, who was now rounding his seat to tend to Elijah. Together, he and Edward gingerly moved Elijah to a comfortable position, and then drove the wagon to the Reverend's cottage.

Eubanks reemerged from his bedroom where Elijah rested and asked, "Who would do such a thing? Elijah is a kind man." He shook his head, then opened the door to the town's doctor who was fetched by Clarence. Marna fretted as she told of her meeting with Elijah and then with Thaddeus Jenkins, watching Sarah's reaction to the story once again. Sarah grew hot, and left the house, with Edward close behind.

"Sarah, what was in the note?"

"It was just a note telling you that my father would not let me leave the house to see you. I was hoping we could meet in Annapolis away from…away from here." She put her face in her hands, and cried. "I didn't want for anyone to get hurt. I just wanted to see you and explain why I reacted so horribly at the Winslow's party. You shocked me, but I realized…I realized that it didn't matter to me who your parents were, and that it was you whom I…."

Edward took her in his arms to comfort her. "Thank you for coming all this way. I see that it is not safe for you to be here. Your father has made that clear with his marks on Elijah."

"But my father would never hurt me…" Sarah began to protest.

"Sarah, you need to return to Wilmington. It is for the best that you and I say goodbye now. I don't want any harm to come to you…."

It was Sarah's turn to cut Edward off. "Now you listen to me, Edward Marshall. I won't let my father tell me what to do, and I certainly won't let you tell me what to do, either. I am coming with you today, and that is final. Marna will stay here and take care of Elijah. She's sweet on him, she told me so on the trip down here this morning. And I am…I am sweet on you," she stammered defiantly, as she pulled away from him. Sarah purposefully walked back to the wagon in front of Eubanks' cottage, reached in and grabbed her bag. Then, facing the dock, she marched toward Edward's ship, but stopped short when she saw the name Edward had painted on the stern.

In an instant, Edward realized the impact. Sarah reeled and shouted, "just who is Anne Marie!?"

"My mother," Edward lowered his head, waiting for a tongue lashing he felt sure would follow.

"Your mother? Well, I guess that's fitting. Surprising, but fitting to pay tribute to her. May I go aboard, now?" Sarah looked at Edward earnestly.

He took three steps toward her, and grabbed her by the arm to lead her aboard. When he had finished giving her a tour of the ship, he pulled her close, but was interrupted by Eubanks' call.

"Edward, Miss Sarah? I think if you are going to leave, now would be a good time to do so." He stood at the top of the boarding plank, but his eyes were on the road, where a fat man astride a chestnut horse was leaning down, talking to someone.

"I think you are about to have company."

Edward and Sarah quickly came up on deck, and made out the figure to be Sarah's father.

"Do you want to do this the right way?" Eubanks asked, as he pulled a small Bible from his coat pocket.

Edward looked at Sarah, and they nodded in unison.

"Then, in the sight of our Lord, God Almighty, I pronounce you Husband and Wife. You may kiss your bride now."

Eubanks shook their hands quickly, threw an extra bag on board, and quickly ran off the boarding plank while Clarence and Jolly ran up. Pell was taking off the bow line and the midship's lines as quickly as he could, while Jolly and Clarence set the sails and pivoted the boat away from the dock.

"What about Elijah?" Edward called to Eubanks, who stood on the dock waving goodbye.

"Oh, I think he is in good hands with Marna, but we will all tend to him. God's speed be with you, my son."

With just a boat length between the stern and the dock, the approaching Thaddeus Jenkins huffed and cussed at Edward. Sarah brazenly waved goodbye to him, and visibly put her arm through Edward's for her father to see that she had made her choice as Edward manned the ship's wheel.

CHAPTER FIFTEEN

The *Anne Marie* made good time down the coast for the next three days. With wide open waters and gentle winds from the west, she progressed along the path Pell charted. His notations on the chart included traditional longitudinal and latitudinal measurements plus and remarks about the water conditions, wind, and cloud formations that could signal a change in weather. Pell was clearly at home on the sea, and despite his rough appearance, he acted a gentleman around Sarah.

"Miss Sarah, I must say, this sailing life seems to agree with you. Why, I remember seeing Edward's own mother at the rail, just as you are now. She was as content as you appear to be." Pell stopped for a moment from writing in his log to gaze at the horizon.

"Tell me more, Mr. Pell. I want to know about Edward's birthplace. Is that where we are going?" She turned fully to face him, her face reddened by the summer sun.

"Aye. Barbados. It is a lovely place, with the whitest beaches you'll ever see, and cliffs. Not like too many of the islands down that way. It's not too far, Missy."

"Tell me about Edward's parents. I mean, I know what they were. But what about *who* they were? Can you tell me what you know?"

"Well, this is not mine to tell, Miss, but I can say that they were both good people in their own ways. Captain Major Stede Bonnet grew mean after Edward's mother passed. I don't think he was the same man after that. I can't rightly say if'n he would have continued with his pirate ways if she lived. It is me opinion that he planned to return to her…otherwise, he wouldn't have left her with so much trea…" Pell caught himself.

"Miss Anne Marie was a kind woman, and a beauty, if'n you don't mind me saying so. I don't think she was partial to anyone else in Barbados except the captain, and she seemed to love to be on the water, just like you."

"I do love being aboard. The wind in the sails, the water racing past the hull…I think I like it best that Edward built this ship. And on it, we begin our life together." Sarah turned to look at the water surging past the side of the ship in rhythmic waves, and then walked aft in search of Edward.

He had been at the helm all morning, steering the course Pell suggested. They would head to windward of many of the Caribbean Islands that were held by foreign governments, and on south toward the Lesser Antilles where Barbados held the eastern-most position. Trade was brisk between islands, and Pell assured Edward that once they reached the Lesser Antilles, they could pick up a cargo for a fee as they weaved their way through the islands to Barbados. They first had to make it over the northerly flowing sea river that separated the colonies from the Caribbean, but Pell explained that if they headed far enough south first, the bumpy ride would be short.

"Edward," Sarah called, one hand on the rail and the other on her skirts. "Are you in need of rest? If you will show me how to read the compass heading, I will steer so you can rest a bit." She put her hand on the compass binnacle, a large brass deck-mounted fixture that stood in front of the helm.

"Thank you for offering, Sarah, but I have a better idea." He called Jolly over. "Jolly, please take the helm while my wife and I go fix some food for us all." Jolly took the helm, and Sarah and Edward went to the galley. "My wife," Edward repeated quietly to Sarah, as he took her in his arms once they were below. "These last few days have been the most exciting days of my life, Sarah, thanks to you. Are you sure you want to continue on with me to the islands? We are not so far out to sea that I can't turn to the west and take you to Charleston. You could stay there, and I would come back for you."

Sarah shook her head.

"How about Savannah? I hear that's a lovely town, too."

Again, Sarah shook her head, and cuddled close to Edward. "No, my place is with you, aboard the *Anne Marie*. And anyway, I've always wanted to go to the islands. Now is a good opportunity for me to see where you are from. Besides, I might be of help when it comes time to get your treasure."

Edward looked dumbfounded. "Treasure?"

"Pell told me. Oh, I don't think he meant to, but it slipped out that your father left something for your mother. And given that Pell has been eager to return to the island all this time, it just makes sense that he was blackmailing you: take him to the islands for the treasure, or he would tell me about your past. You spoiled his surprise, trying to be honorable and all, but now that the truth is out, I might be able to help you get it, if you will tell me where it is and what we are looking for."

Edward wasn't sure if he should be pleased with her for being so clever, or mad at Pell for being so dumb. Anyway, she did have a point, it might be helpful to have a woman around to help get them onto the grounds where Pell claimed the shed was.

But before he could answer her, Jolly called out.

"Ship astern, gaining fast!"

Edward and Sarah ran on deck and took their places beside Clarence and Pell who held a scope to his eye. A ship with six full sails was coming along the same course. Larger than the *Anne Marie*, the ship had no flags flying.

"This is not good," Pell stated quietly. "They have guns. Lots of guns. We only have three cannon."

"Do you mean they are looking for a fight?" asked Sarah with an excited expression on her face.

"In the old days, we ran without our flags as we approached ships, hoping they would slow down so as to get a good look at us. That was surely to our advantage. By the time we caught up with them, we'd send our colors up the mast, and it was too late for them to outrun us." Pell was calculating wind and distance in his head now. "If we stay on our current course, we could have a smooth ride for two days or so, until we hit the north sea river. But if that ship is after us, they will catch up with us here in the flat waters. If we turn seaward now, we will hit the rough waters by nightfall. We could let the river carry us further to the north, and then we could keep heading easterly to Bermuda, wait it out a few weeks, and then head south again."

"Pell, did you tell *anyone else* our destination?" Edward scolded.

"No, not that I remember," Pell looked chastened. I didn't tell no one in Wilmington, so if'n that ship is coming after us, it's not because they know what we are going after. It's more likely because of who we have aboard." He nodded at Sarah. "Or it might be a slave ship. They might be out looking for a fresh load. Hard to tell this far away. I don't know if you want to tangle with them either way, Edward."

"Very well. Clarence, alter course due east. Jolly, you and Pell get those sails full and by. I will help you. Sarah, go below and get the horns of gun powder. If they want to fight, we'll fight. Maybe they are not after us at all, but either way, we are ready."

All hands aboard the small vessel did Edward's bidding. Edward worried about how solid his ship was for only a minute. He'd built it for coastal cruising and not for long sea passages, but with Clarence's experience as a helmsmen and Pell's navigational skills, they would soon find out her merit. For the rest of the day, they kept at the ready, watching the ship to the stern stay its course. It was soon clear that the ship was in pursuit of the *Anne Marie*.

Just as Pell had promised, the ride grew bumpy in frantic swells of the northerly river. Clarence was at the helm when they entered the swift currents, and adeptly steered for all he was worth to make the most of it. Clarence knew these waters well, so he was ready for the waves that pushed the *Anne Marie* hard. Jolly, Edward, and Sarah did not fare so well as they tried to manage the lines, but Pell embraced the race, as he called it.

"This is more like it!" Pell shouted at no one in particular in the darkness of the new night. Once they reached the roughest part of the river, Pell doused the ship's lights. "If'n they try and follow us, they won't find us." Meanwhile, he kept an eye out for the other ship's lights, first visible then gone from sight as the *Anne Marie* moved in the pitching waves. Pell and Clarence alternated between helm and lookout posts, while the others huddled below--or ran up on deck to the rail. Each person had a rope tied around the waist to keep the short-handed crew from falling overboard into confused swells.

By midmorning, the *Anne Marie* hit calmer waters. Still gray from the choppy passage, Edward and Sarah gingerly made their way up on deck for fresh air, and to survey the waters behind them. There was no sign of the other ship.

"Shall we keep on to Bermuda, or head south?" Edward called to a weary Pell, who lounged on the deck behind the helm while Clarence stretched his legs. Jolly was making his way forward to set sails right and tidy up the lines again.

"Well, let's see. Are we all alone, again?" Pell got to his knees, then pulled himself up to the aft railing. After viewing through his eyeglass, he declared they had escaped their pursuers, and stated that south would be the way to go. "Soon, we will find the trade winds, and they will help us to the south. We will have to make our way to the Leeward Islands, then go on south to the Windward Islands and Barbados." He went forward to his cabin to get his chart and sextant so he could pinpoint exactly where they were.

Relieved, Edward and Sarah took over steering so Clarence could rest. Jolly offered to fix something to eat for them all, and the day looked as if it would be fair for sailing to the islands, now an extra week away. Edward calculated if he had enough provisions to last until they reached the northernmost of the Leeward Islands. It would be close, but fish could be had along the way, and they could catch rainwater to drink if the barrels started to ring hollow. Still rolling a bit, the *Anne Marie* would sail faster with assistance of the trade winds to come.

But Fate would not be so kind that day. In a few hours' time, Sarah spotted the sails again on the horizon. This time, there was a flag flying in the breeze. A long, steady look through the eyepiece, and Sarah's heart sank. A gold arrow piercing a circle of red end shone clearly against its dark green background, identifying it as one of her father's ships. In a few short hours, it closed the distance between the two ships, and Edward again prepared his crew and ship for battle.

By late afternoon, the other ship was four ship lengths behind. A cannon thundered, and the resulting splash rolled the *Anne Marie* from side to side.

"I cannot believe they would fire on us, knowing Sarah is aboard!" Edward was petrified. "What do they think they are doing?"

Pell was quick to respond. "That shot was just to get your attention. I suspect they want to board you and take her home. The way I see it, you got two choices. You can let them do that, and you would surely be killed if Jenkins has his way; or you can fight. This is your ship. You want them to sink 'er?"

"No I do not! I'll be damned if I am going to let Jenkins or any other man take from me the two things that mean the most. Pell, I must rely now on your fighting expertise."

"Edward, I only know how to fight as a pirate, not as a gentleman."

"Then we shall fight as pirates," Edward said calmly. "You have the command." He bowed slightly.

"Ready the cannon, Jolly," Pell beamed. "We are coming about. Clarence, you are to hold us steady. Jolly, when we get within three ship's lengths of that ship, fire at their bow first. If they advance, light the second cannon, Edward, and then get the third cannon ready. That may be our only chance. Miss Sarah, do you know how to shoot?"

"Yes, Mr. Pell. I've had some practice hunting quail in Maryland," Sarah stood tall and proud.

"Well, we are now a-hunting, Missy. Get your guns ready. There are four in my cabin. I brought extras aboard, just in case." Pell winked at her. "If you see something getting close enough to hit, fire."

All hands scrambled over the deck, and Pell relished his role as commander of the *Anne Marie*. They were as ready as they ever would be when the other ship closed in and stood off three boat lengths away.

Jolly lit the first cannon, and missed their bow by a wide margin. He repacked it as quickly as he could while Edward lit a fuse on the second one. Edward's shot hit the bowsprit of the other ship at the same time she fired her cannon. The cannon ball rocked the *Anne Marie*, grazing her mizzen mast. After a quick survey of what little damage it had caused, Edward packed his cannon with powder and another cannonball. They didn't have very many as each one was costly, but what they had on board would have to do.

"Steady, steady. Clarence, push a little to the outside, if you would please. We have to get a clear shot at her amidships. I am guessing by her size that in her belly there lies the cargo hold filled with gunpowder," Pell said, pointing to the center of the ship. "It would be a pity to waste her, but we can't very well handle two ships with such a small crew," Pell smiled at the thought of taking the ship as his own. "No matter, she shall have to go down." Jolly, are you ready?"

"Yes sir!" Jolly snapped. For all his fifteen years, he looked and acted the part of a well-seasoned crewman. He had told Edward when he joined the crew that he wanted to become a merchant marine, and he was eager to get aboard any ship for experience. Surely this was more experience than any teen needed, but he seemed to be up for the task.

"Wait for my signal," Pell leaned over him to ensure his cannon was positioned to the greatest strategic advantage.

After Sarah laid a gun at Clarence's feet, she took her post next to the remaining three guns on the aft deck. She aimed her gun steadily on the railing. While the gun was almost as big as she, Sarah knew that leveraging it with the railing would help her get a clear shot off if she had a chance. She trusted Pell's instructions, as did the rest of the crew. But more importantly, she believed in Edward and in their future together. She was fighting for her future, and she decided she would defend her choice or die trying.

"Steady," Pell put his hand on Jolly's shoulder who prepared the fuse for lighting. When the other ship inched forward, Pell instructed Jolly to wait until he could see the midsection just coming into view through the cannon's port in the *Anne Marie's* hull.

But before Jolly could light the fuse, the other ship shot a cannon ball into the side of the *Anne Marie*, and her rolling motion at impact threw Jolly and Pell off their feet and to the other side of the ship!

Edward raced to them, and Pell waved him off to say he was alright. Jolly, though tossed and bruised, was not injured. Edward quickly looked over the side of his hull and saw that the hit ripped into the wood just above the waterline. He looked up at Sarah and Clarence, who were shaken but still at the ready.

Sarah moved on hands and knees to Edward's unattended cannon, and got the fuse ready as she had just seen Jolly do.

Edward dashed for the torch, and lit the fuse. The cannon arched back after it released it shot…a shot that hit the center of the other ship squarely amidships. Just as Pell had predicted, a catastrophic fire blew much of the deck off and crewmembers into the water. The ship's main mast crumbled with the blast and took sails and rigging for the other masts with it.

"Good on you, Edward! Congratulations, Missy!" Pell was elated. "You've officially *taken* your first ship. A finer pair of pirates I have never seen."

Clarence steered away from the sinking ship in the dwindling daylight, and Jolly found his feet again. He scampered below to assess the damage, and smartly reported to Edward the location and size of the hole. Edward, Sarah and Pell dashed below and grabbed Edward's table and benches, ripping them apart quickly and securing the hole in the side of the ship with the planks. Pell suggested they get one of the sails from the other ship as an extra measure of coverage, but Edward declined.

"What we've done here is enough to hold her for now. In the morning, I will get the pitch ready, and go over the side to smooth it into the new planks. Jolly, in my cabin are some more timbers. At first light, we will bring those topside and measure for a proper fitting. Meanwhile, if everyone agrees, we should offer assistance to any crew member wanting it on that ship."

"Begging your pardon, Edward, but that is probably not a good idea." Pell crossed his arms to show his displeasure.

"We can't just leave them here, Pell. They will freeze overnight and die."

"I believe that is what they had in mind for you, my friend. If you carry them with you, they will know your whereabouts wherever you go, and surely get word back to Mr. Jenkins. He doesn't seem like the sort of man who gives up easily."

Edward looked at Sarah. Then he went topside, and found the eyepiece. The other ship was still floating, and crew members who could were slowly making their way back aboard what was left of their damaged ship. Many bodies were in the water – the ones who would never see the break of day. Satisfied that the ship could flounder for a few days until they reached Bermuda, Edward told Clarence to set a course for the islands.

Sarah came up on deck, and together she and Edward turned their backs on the other ship's remains and all it represented for good.

Chapter Sixteen

"It's so beautiful, Edward!" Sarah was amazed at the verdant hills and valleys surrounded by turquoise and paler blue waters of the Caribbean Islands.

Ribbons of white bordered lush maritime forests on many of the islands, yet clusters of land in the smaller island groups varied widely from the large volcanic masses that rose from the same Caribbean Sea, offering little protection from the open ocean's seas. Many islands in the northern part of the chain known as the Bahamas were porous deposits of limestone laced with deep blue holes and coral mounds. Further south, there were outcroppings of small islands where tall volcanic mountains commanded the attention of the crew with their majestic beauty.

"Do you remember any of this?" Sarah asked Edward as she slipped her hand through his arm.

"Not really. What memories I have of Barbados are not fond, so this is refreshing to look at the islands as an adult." He pulled Sarah close. "I am glad to share it with you. It makes the journey easier."

Weaving their way through the islands, the crew of the *Anne Marie* found much needed rest in sheltered harbors where Edward quickly made a strong patch that covered the hole ripped by the cannonball. Along the way, they also found small amounts of cargo for inter-island trading that helped pay for stores for the remainder of the voyage, and a small bonus for Pell, Jolly, and Clarence. Edward was a fair captain who wanted to retain his crew, but also wanted them to know him as an honest captain who valued them and their efforts. Sarah's respect and understanding of him as a captain and husband grew as well, and she likewise gained the admiration of all aboard for her equally valiant efforts during the many weeks at sea.

The ports that they visited were as varied as the islands themselves. Some had well-defined ballast stone streets and townships holding handsome buildings surrounded by lush plants and gardens of equally groomed homes. Other islands, some not more than small spits of sand or atolls, were uninhabited, where jungles spilled out of their boundaries to white or pink beaches sequestered in protected coves.

There in the lee of the islands, Edward anchored for a night or two. And while Sarah and Edward were familiar with the stifling heat of the Carolina coast during the summer time, it did little to prepare them for the heat they felt here. It was hot and humid, and what little breeze stirred through the trees was mildly warm, too. But it was blessedly constant.

To take advantage of it, Clarence and Jolly rigged a canvas shade on deck, securing it fore and aft and across the beam of the ship to offer protection from the sun. At night, they would sleep on deck under the canvas, and occasionally, the others would join them to enjoy cooler air topside.

During the day, as the *Ann Marie* picked her way through the islands, Jolly and Clarence took turns at the helm and at the forward deck on the lookout for the often present coral heads that sometimes bloomed into the deeper channels. Along the coast of the New World, it was rocks or shoals. Coral heads were just as dangerous and in some cases more so because shipping channels were not well defined in the islands.

Pressing toward their goal, Edward and his crew often enjoyed time for fishing for fresh food or foraging through villages for fruits and some vegetables. Sarah even learned to use whatever food sources she could find in the less inhabited islands to make scrumptious meals. As Sarah had never had the need to learn to cook in the colonies, this was as much a learning experience for her as it was for the crew who tested what she cooked in varying conditions as they voyaged. By the time they approached Bridgetown's harbor entrance, she was well practiced with biscuits, various fish dishes and even some chutney sauces to add a little flavor to an otherwise repetitive fare.

Pell seemed instantly younger the day the *Anne Marie* made anchor in Bridgetown's harbor. He set about his tasks with unusual haste, and even volunteered to assist

Clarence and Jolly with their chores so they could make their way ashore. That particular day was clear, and as Edward began to set a tender in the water, Pell jumped to assist him. Up until this day, not much had been said of the treasure…or a plan by which to secure it. But Pell offered several ideas about gaining access to the grounds: under cover of darkness, which was ruled out by Edward; scale the cliffs unnoticed at the back of the property, which was ruled out by Sarah; boldly walk in, lay claim and take what they wanted, an idea which met with a resounding "no" from Edward and Sarah in unison.

"Well then, how to you think we should do it, pray tell?" said an agitated Pell to Edward and Sarah as he rowed them into Bridgetown about midday in the small dinghy.

Edward was still trying to lay out a conversation with the customs officers regarding his route, his ship, and his cargo hold, which was full of bananas from the French-held island of St. Lucia. Because Edward was considered a colonist, he and his crew met with some hostilities whenever they entered French ports, but because they served as merchants carrying valuable cargo between the islands, they were unharmed.

"Once we clear customs, Sarah and I will head for the merchant office of…Sarah, was is the fellow's name?" He turned to Sarah as she brought a small black journal from her bag.

"Oliver St. Andres, the Frenchman," she said from memory as she flipped through the logbook containing notes on past cargos and deliveries. She had become accustomed to listening for the details of every transaction, and made notations as soon as Edward returned from other merchant offices. When cargo came aboard, she noted the quantity and general quality, and summed up the same, including losses, so they could learn which cargos lasted between islands.

"Yes, that is what the man in St. Lucia said. 'Look for de man in the white shack nearest de far left side of de harbor'," she did her best to imitate the banana merchant.

"Right," Edward smiled at her cleverness. "Once we make arrangements to offload the bananas, Clarence and Jolly will see to their delivery. Then we will make our way to the place where you think the jewels are."

He turned a quizzical eye to Pell. "Pell, there will be no skullduggery here, am I understood?"

"Of course not, Edward. No, I think we should just walk up to the front door, introduce ourselves and have a looksey about the place." Pell turned away in disgust. After regaining his valor as a pirate at sea, the last thing he wanted to pretend to be was a *gentleman*.

"Pell, I am thinking that Sarah and I will go to the house alone, and when we are able to gain access and create a distraction to the owners, then you make your way around the property as quickly as you can without drawing attention to yourself. If someone asks about you, I will say you just want to stretch your legs, or something like it. Just be sure to keep the shovel out of sight."

Pell tapped the dingy canvas bag beside him. "I think I shall be able to disguise it."

"Very well. But you mustn't be too long. I don't want to cause any suspicion, Pell."

Pell nodded as he pulled the last few stroked on the oars.

Edward turned slightly to face the approaching dock to hold on while Pell climbed out and secured the tender to the dock across from the white customs house. Edward then helped Sarah out of the tender and hoisted himself out while she tucked a stray hair up in her yellow bonnet and smoothed a well-worn blue dress as best she could.

Edward and Sarah crossed the cobblestone street to the customs house while Pell waited at the tender. When Edward and Sarah emerged from the cool interior of the house onto the wide shaded porch, the three then made their way to the far side of the harbor, Pell by tender, and Edward and Sarah on foot. Along the way, Sarah went into a small stucco-sided bakery, and Edward continued to the warehouse of Oliver St. Andres.

The warehouse looked and smelled like many of the others Edward had been in during the last few months: a dark interior punctuated by the light from large opening bay doors, where cargo of various descriptions was wheeled in or out at a fast clip. Horse droppings added to the stench of overripe fruit rotting in tropical heat, and the mixture was something between repugnant and sweet. In the middle of one end was the tall stand of the warehouse's master, whose high seat and table took best advantage of whatever breeze was available. The din of the place was familiar to Edward, and the cadence of horses and mules' hooves on the half-planked floor set the pace for the day's activities there.

"I am looking for a Mr. St. Adres," Edward called to the tall man sitting up on a high stool.

"Oui, you have found heem," said the man, as he wiped sweat off of his round spectacles and forehead. His angular jaw and high pointy nose were at complete opposite to his wildly curly hair that was loosely gathered in a red ribbon. "And who might you bee?" He pointed his feathered quill at Edward.

"Edward Marshall, at your service. I've cargo for you from St. Lucia. A friend of yours said you would be interested, and that I should contact you first."

"St. Lucia? Oui, I suspect this to bee bananas from Jean Norvue?" He put his glasses back on, then slid them up onto the mass of curls above his forehead, still glowing with sweat.

"Yes," said Edward, as he offered papers of the transaction in St. Lucia. In a few minutes, business was complete, and Mr. St. Andres sent two of his men in the direction of the wharf to row out to the *Anne Marie*.

Edward packed his papers and earnings tightly into his billfold, and then slid it into the inside pocket of the vest that Mrs. Kelly so cleverly designed. It had come in handy, making Edward feel secure in carrying valuables discreetly while looking respectable in the many warehouses and wharves he'd visited through the islands on the voyage to Barbados. Often, the heat prohibited more formal attire but a man dressed in a vest was respected in these parts, Edward soon learned.

He met Sarah as she emerged from a shop along the waterfront, her arms laden with packages of fabric, long bread loaves and a basket of fresh fruit from the market. Edward helped her with her packages, and the two made their way toward Pell and the waiting tender.

"In heaven's name, woman, why have you bought fruit? Surely it will spoil in this heat," Pell was clearly agitated as he grabbed the basket of kiwis and limes from Sarah.

"If we are to go visiting, we would be better received if we come bearing gifts," Sarah retorted, "I dare say that anyone would mistake that gesture for anything less than proper. Besides, it is too late in the day to go calling. We should set out again early tomorrow." She straightened her bonnet, and gingerly stepped into the tender. Edward nodded his approval of her sensibilities, and Pell snorted as he took his place at the oars again, rowing them from the main wharf back to the ship.

"According to your calculations, Pell, we should get an early start anyway to make the tide," Edward tried to calm Pell. "Can we go over the route again?"

"In the morning, we will weigh anchor and sail back out into the Atlantic Ocean, just inside Cobbler's Reef and anchor in Crane's Bay," Pell said between pulls on the oars. "From there, we will do best to make our way quickly through the little town that lies just at the water's edge, and then up the path I told you about that will take us to the higher ground." Pell was gaining his confidence as navigator again. "Our trip will have to be a quick one," Pell noted. "The waters inside Cobbler's Reef feel the same tides and currents as the Atlantic Ocean that it guards the coast from. If we wait too long to get out, we might return to a dangerously low tide. At best, we have less than six hours between tides: four hours on a rising tide plus two hours of flat water before the tide began its race back out to open water."

The tidal range for the island was about four to six feet, enough to set the *Anne Marie* on her side in a hurry if they lingered in shallow waters. Being inside a reef then became extremely dangerous, because the ship would be exposed to sharp coral heads.

"Once we make it to the edge of St. Philips Parish, I can show you the main road that leads to the cottage," Pell continued. "You take whatever basket of goods or trinkets you want to the front of the house, and I will wait for a few minutes before I make me way toward the back of the property. I trust that you can gain the confidence of whoever opens the door to you. Can you do some sort of bird call? Can you whistle like this?" Pell let out a shrill whistle, first low, then high pitched.

Edward made a similar sound, and Sarah laughed at the two of them, and then chimed in with her best imitation of their warbling birdcalls.

"Right, then. That will be the signal that either you can't get in, or you are done," said Pell. "When I hear you make that call, we'll consider our time as run out, and meet back at path at the top of the cliffs."

"How will you make it to the shed without being seen?" Sarah quizzed.

"Unless it's changed, there is thick brush that boarders the property…oleander, I think it's called. I can make my way unnoticed through much of it. The property backs up to the top of the cliffs, and at some points, the cliff forms a wall to the edge of the land. If I need to, I might be able to crawl along the edge."

"It sounds like you want to do it the hard way, Pell," Edward noted, as they reached the ship. "You could just walk up with us, but stay outside. I can say that you are our guide to the house. Then you could just walk around the property to stretch your legs, and slip out of sight of the house."

"Too easy," Pell shook his head. "No, if we are going to have an adventure, let's have us a big one." Pell smiled mischievously. He clearly had been thinking about his return for a long time, so Edward agreed not to spoil his fun.

That evening, under the canopy on deck, a gentle breeze cooled the crew. Over a good supper of fresh meat, fruit, bread and a bit of rum for Pell, Edward and Sarah dreamed up conversations with the occupants of the chattel cottage.

Clarence and Jolly would stay aboard in case they needed to move the ship out of the reef. They knew this was a special trip through the reef, though they did not know the nature of the business that was at hand. In any event, they agreed to follow Pell's instructions, and were ready to get underway early the following morning before the sun peaked over the horizon.

The wind was with them as the *Anne Marie* rounded South Point, the southernmost cropping of silvery beach on the island. It would take the better part of three hours to get to Crane's Bay, Pell said, so to make the cut inside the reef on the rising tide, they needed to sail as fast as they could up the coast. When they dropped the anchor at the mouth of the bay, Edward and Jolly lowered the tender over the side, and Sarah, in her freshest dress and bonnet, made her way over the gunwale to the small craft below. Pell even had the good sense to clean up, just in case he needed to be presentable, he said. Edward rowed Sarah and Pell to shore, noting that Pell would have to conserve his strength for his part of the adventure.

It was ten o'clock when he landed the tender on the beach that morning, and helped Sarah to shore first before pulling the boat on the beach and tying its line to a mangrove tree. Unlike Bridgetown, this village was small though a port town. A few shops in small cottages well off the strip of pale beach intermingled with larger stone cottages and homes that seemed to get lost in a tangle of vines and trees. A sand path lined with shells was the only way one could pass through the lush growth, but the majority of the town sat up on the top of the cliff. A large wooden crane lifted cargo from the beach to the top of the cliffs, offering clues to how the village and bay got their name.

"We must be back here to get the ship out of the reef not later than two o'clock this afternoon," Pell instructed. Edward, keep an eye on your watch, I haven't one, so I must depend on you to keep us on schedule."

"I will make the call if we are getting close to the time," Edward nodded, patting the watch pocket of his vest. The three wasted no time in the village and headed for the path that Pell assured them would lead them to the top of the cliffs.

Pell seemed energized with every step up the steep path, so he set a quick pace for the others to follow even as he carried his canvas bag containing the tools he would need for his chore.

Sarah clutched her small sweet grass basket of bread and fruit that she planned to give to the mistress of the house as she walked briskly to keep up with Pell and Edward.

When they finally stopped for a sip of water at the top of the ridge, Pell looked around and smiled with delight. "It's all the same! This is where we part company, and where we need to meet again in a few hours. See that cottage over there with the bougainvillea twisting up that trellis? That's the place," Pell pointed an expanded chattel house. "I never thought I would see it again, but there it is. That is the house where you was born, Edward. Right there, in that room that faces the road. I can still remember as if it was only yesterday..." Pell removed his hat for a moment of reverence to Edward's mother. "Now you go, and be quick about it," he placed his battered hat back on his head, and turned away from the front entrance to the house just a few feet away. "Just remember the call." With that, he was off at a brisk pace along the top of the cliff and disappeared in the thick oleander and other lush growth.

Edward put on his coat that he had taken off for their climb up the path, then held out his hand to Sarah. Together they paced themselves as they approached the whitewashed gate that opened to a small garden filled with hibiscus and tropical "Bird of Paradise" plants. Tendrils of brilliant pink and red bougainvillea wrapped around every upright porch column, and then across the red tiled roof.

With some hesitancy, Edward knocked on the pale blue door, while Sarah stood just behind him on the porch. For all their planning, he suddenly lost the words he wanted to say.

He turned to Sarah with the thought of leaving at once, before anyone knew they had ever entered the property. Before he could open his mouth, the door opened. A small-framed woman in her sixties smiled at Edward and Sarah.

"Yes?" Her voice was high, and full of energy. Seeing Edward's hesitation, Sarah brushed past Edward hurriedly to make a proper introduction.

"Good morning, Ma'am. Please forgive our intrusion, but my husband and I have come quite a long way to see this house where he was born. My name is Sarah, and this Edward Marshall. May we trouble you for minute?"

"Born here? In this house? Oh my, dear, yes, do come in," she opened the door wide. Pleasant smells of cooking spices wafted out the door, beckoning the visitors inside.

The old lady ambled slowly ahead. "I came upon this house many years ago when I first arrived on the island. It was a shambles, but I loved the overrun garden here and in the back." The woman gestured to chairs in what passed as a parlor, and then seated herself opposite Sarah and Edward. "My name is Esther Montgomery, and I am so pleased to have company," she smiled broadly. She called for her maid.

"Jasmine, bring us something cold, will you please?" Just as politely, she turned to Edward. "Tell me about your family."

Edward squirmed at her directness, and Sarah piped up. "Edward tells me that his family moved away when he was but a small boy. When did you say you moved to Barbados, Mrs. Montgomery?"

"Oh, please call me Esther. My husband passed away about ten years ago, so I decided to come here to escape that nasty winter weather in London. I had no family there, but once my husband, Wiley we called him, passed away, there was no reason to stay. I really had just planned on traveling a bit, and of course, I wanted to see Barbados because my brother had been through here some years earlier. I hoped to find him, but he had already left. I remember the day I saw this place. I wanted to get the highest point of this side of the island. Back in those days, it was so much quieter than Bridgetown. I planned to see if I could view any of the islands to the south, or to the north, and then decide which way to go next on my travels. But while walking to the high point of the cliffs that lie across the road in front, I fell and twisted my ankle. I was alone--a foolish thing to do, but I was so accustomed to my independence after my husband passed. I soon found that I could hobble only a little bit before it hurt, so I made my way to the gate outside this home. It was about fallen in I tell you, but I had hopes that there would be someone home who could help me."

Jasmine entered the room and placed a silver tray on the small table to the side of Esther. She then offered tall glasses of juice to Edward and Sarah, and gave Esther her glass. The elderly negress curtseyed and left the room, humming softly.

Esther continued her tale. "As I said, it was quite a ramshackle, with bougainvillea growing everywhere, and the gate torn off its hinges. But there was humming coming from inside. Soft, you know, gentle, like what you just heard. I limped to the front door, and Jasmine opened it and her home to me. She cared for my ankle then, and she has been caring for me ever since. She is nearly blind, but she knows this house well enough to care for it daily. I dare say I would not have stayed on the island had it not been for her kindness."

Edward regained his voice as Esther told her story. He saw the main room's furnishings, and tried to imagine the

room in his father's day. Were these the same chairs? He
didn't quite know how to phrase his questions, but one in
particular burned in his mind until he thought it might
spill out of his mouth: was Jasmine one of the women
who cared for him as a baby? He searched his mind for
any hint to the description of her that Pell might have
offered that night in the tavern. But he could remember
nothing that would satisfy him. He stayed alert to Esther's story, all the while keeping an ear out for Pell who
was touring the property's perimeter at this very minute.

"The gardens are my favorite part about the house,"
continued Esther. I have taken great care in bringing
them back to life after much neglect. Jasmine, bless her
heart, is somewhat confined to the house due to her poor
eyesight, but she has shared with me many, many stories of what they used to look like. Before I came along,
she had been taking in boarders from time to time, to
help with the general upkeep of the house and to earn a
meager wage. We still offer shelter to wayward travelers,
and God willing, they are able to offer a little tithing for
our troubles; but my pension takes care of our living ex-
penses mostly. My late husband, God rest his soul, was a
very astute businessman and he has provided well for me
in my old age. Where are you staying on the island, and
how long will you be here?"

"We are going to stay aboard our ship," Edward focused in
on the conversation at hand again. "We are quite comfortable
aboard, and it is easier if one of the merchants in town needs
to reach us to arrange for a cargo trade. That is how we've

come to this island, by way of trade. We will be heading back to the colonies once we get a full hold."

"Well then certainly you will want to meet a Mr. James Bonnet. He owns this house as well as the largest warehouse in Bridgetown, and is an exporter of sugar cane and other goods," explained Esther. "Most anyone in town can direct you to his warehouse, but I am told that he spends most of his days on his plantation. His health is failing. Why, Mr. Marshall, you look as if you have seen a ghost! Are you ill?"

Esther reached out her hand to Edward as he snapped his hands to his head. Sarah intervened.

"Headaches. My husband gets terrible headaches sometimes. Dear, perhaps you need to get some fresh air?" She slowly stood and helped Edward to his feet, gently pulling him toward the door. "I am sorry to break our visit, Esther, you have been most kind to see us today," she looked over Esther's shoulder toward a window, hoping to get a quick view of the garden or shed. She had no idea where Pell was, but felt sure their time was almost up.

Esther stood with her, and helped Edward to the door. "Are you sure fresh air is good? I would think he would want to rest."

"I will be fine in a few minutes," Edward said, "in fact, I am feeling better already. I hope we have not kept you too long visiting."

"Oh, what is time to an old woman?" Esther brightened, seeing that Edward's color was coming back to his face. "We don't even have a clock here, and it suits me. I have no idea what time it is."

Edward pulled out his pocket watch from his vest, and opened the case to check the time. They had but a few minutes left before they would have to leave for the ship to catch the tide before it fell. "It is approaching…"

"That watch. Where did you get that watch? Esther broke in, her eyes wide, her stance frozen.

"It was a gift…a gift from a very dear friend of mine," Edward answered.

"That watch is the same one that my father gave to my brother before he entered the ministry." Esther reached gingerly for the watch, and Edward released it to her. "I have been looking for him for years, and he seemed always to be two steps ahead of me. Whenever I think I've found him again, he moves on. I have tried to keep up with him, and Barbados is the last place that has record of him being. That's what brought me here, only I arrived nearly ten years too late. And now, after all these years, I find yet another link to where he is. Where are you from, Edward?"

Jasmine came into the room hearing the alarm in her mistress's voice. She stood very close to her in a protective way.

Edward took a deep breath, and thought quickly of how to tell Esther about the Reverend without giving away his own past. "The watch was given to me by the Reverend Jonathan Eubanks. I knew him in Brunswick, just south of the Virginia colony. He has retired from ministry, but he is very much a fixture in the community there. He has had great impact on my life over many years, but he didn't share that much about his own family. I presumed he was an orphan, like myself."

"Orphan? Oh, heavens no!" Esther laughed, and gave Edward his watch back. Jasmine excused herself, hearing her mistress relax again. "Jonathan was one the youngest of four brothers--and my baby brother. There was a fire when we were young, and my mother and two of my brothers were lost. So my father raised the rest of us. Samuel was the oldest, then me, and then there was Jonathan. Samuel married early in life, and he and his family moved to the country. When I married, my father and my older brother turned their backs on me. You see, my husband was not from a good family. His parents were very poor, and my father always thought I could do better. But I was in love, so I married without his blessing. Jonathan married us, and encouraged us to get back into Father's good graces before he set off for an assignment. I was never sure where he was going in those days."

"My husband and I traveled quite a bit and I lost touch with my brother. When I got word that my father died, I was ashamed. I tried to find Jonathan, but wasn't sure where to start. The Church was of little help, because once he left one parish, they would not continue to track where his next duty was. He was...in the eyes of the Church, he was somewhat of an odd duck. I think it is because he tried secular life first. But after Jonathan's own wife died, he took his only child and entered the ministry hoping to make amends for whatever sins he thought had brought such tragedy to his own life."

Edward stood amazed. Eubanks had been married? "What became of his child? Did it...live?"

"Oh, yes. For a few years, anyway. Jonathan tried his best to make a home for the poor little girl. Rosie was her name, after her mother. But he really was not capable of caring for her as an infant and before long, she fell ill and died before her fourth birthday. It was a sad, sad time. Once his rage was gone, Jonathan decided to dedicate his life to helping other children live better. His ministry was to children at first, and but the church kept pushing him to reach adults. It was so frustrating to him, so he took appointments in locations far away from the city. I lost touch with him after a while.

"Then, my husband passed away in the same year that our older brother, Samuel, was killed. I wanted to let Jonathan know, so I set out to look for him. Seeing this watch lets me know that at least he is alive. Come back in, and please tell me about my brother. I want to hear everything!" Esther was emphatic.

Edward quickly glanced at Sarah, then shook his head. "We really need to get back to our ship to move her before the tide goes out. But we can come back another day if you wish, and talk more."

"Oh, yes, yes, do. And in return for your kind words about my brother, I will introduce to whomever you would like to meet here so that you may fill your cargo hold. Please promise that you will come back again."

Edward and Sarah nodded their heads at the same time, and bade Esther goodbye for the day.

They hurried to the trailhead, where Pell sat filing his nails and looking perturbed.

"And while you was in there having tea, I was out there digging in the heat of that damn shed," he steamed. "The least you could do was get here on time." He motioned to a small bundle near the base of the rocks at his feet.

"Sorry, Pell, we couldn't just leave. Did you get what you wanted?" Edward started to reach for the sealed bundle.

"Not so fast, there Mate. I said I would share, and I keep me word. Here is your part." Pell pointed to another bundle placed a little higher up on the rocks.

"Well, well, well. You are a man of your word, Pell. Thank you." Edward reached for his share.

"You can thank me later. We don't have time now. You need to get to the ship now. I will go 'round to Bridgetown to secure proper lodging while you and the others bring the ship out the same way you got in the reef. Then, I can meet you there. We can have a decent meal. No offense to your cookin', Miss Sarah."

"None taken, Pell. I could use a proper meal, too." She looked at Edward, and started down the path.

Edward started to follow. He took a hard look at the still closed bundle, and tossed it back to a stunned Pell. "You keep it, Pell. I have no use for blood money. You got what you came for and I think I have, too. Enjoy your retirement." Edward tipped his hat to Pell, and turned down the path.

Before he was out of earshot, Edward heard Pell whine, "you make it damn difficult for me to be a pirate. Your bundle is filled with banana leaves and rocks!" Edward smiled. He had guessed that would be its contents. He was still glad to leave it, and Pell, behind.

CHAPTER SEVENTEEN

Heading back to open water from behind the reef was a simple matter of picking their way through the opening under short sail just as they had come in, Edward found. For all his failings, Pell was an expert navigator, and his skills would be missed. Pell knew the waters of the Caribbean like he knew the back of his course hands; but without him, Edward and his crew would rely on charts and dead reckoning for the rest of their travels.

That night aboard the *Anne Marie* was quiet. Once at anchor in Bridgetown's wide harbor, Jolly and Clarence rowed to the docks to stretch their legs. Sarah and Edward enjoyed a quiet meal of fresh fish that Jolly had caught while he and Clarence stayed aboard behind the reef--he found the fishing there excellent, he said, and he caught more than he and Clarence could eat for their lunch.

"Edward, dear, you've hardly touched your meal," Sarah broke the silence that had consumed Edward since they boarded the ship earlier that day.

"I am sorry, Sarah, I have been thinking about all that Esther told us…and all that I still do not know."

"What do you mean?"

Edward shifted in his seat, straddling the bench to face her. "If I tell my half-brother who I am, it may spoil everything. I don't want to stake a claim for any of his holdings…"

"But you do, Edward. You want to stake a claim for some of his attention, and hopefully, an acknowledgement that you and he are kin." Sarah was blunt, but her assessment was correct. As she cleared the table and moved gingerly to the galley sink to wash the dishes, she continued talking to Edward over her shoulder. "It seems to me that if a long-lost relative showed up on my door, I would be very curious about that person's life, just as I am sure he would be interested in mine. There's absolutely nothing wrong with that. In fact, I would want to know everything about that person's past, and learn about what separated us."

"But what if that past is the one thing he can't forgive? I mean, he may not even know about me. I would have lived my whole life without knowing of him had the Reverend not told me out of his feelings of guilt."

"Edward, the past is the past," said Sarah emphatically. "You can't change that. The only thing that you can control is your reaction to it. If you continue to let your past--or your father's, for that matter--hold you back from doing what you want, then you will have regrets in years to come. It is easier to live with the things you've done, even if they were not the best choices, than to have regrets staring you in the face on a daily basis. Does that make sense?"

Edward thought for a long while. He got up from the table, and walked to the pot-bellied stove and absentmindedly checked on the fire. This was the same well-used stove that he brought aboard from his home in Brunswick. Sarah fluttered about the galley as if she'd been cooking in there her whole life. She had certainly made the voyage enjoyable, and in some respects, her presence had helped him to understand why his father had allowed his mother to remain aboard for the many months before they returned to Barbados.

"I will go and introduce myself to James tomorrow. His reaction will determine our course as 'kin', but at least I will have done what I have come all this way to do." Edward held out his hand to Sarah, and she accompanied him to the deck to enjoy the night's starry mantle.

The following day bloomed as so many of them did in the islands: pale yellow and pink gave way to an azure blue in the sky that matched the blue of the deeper water in the harbor.

Sarah declined the papaya and fresh bread that Jolly offered her at breakfast, saying she was still full from last night's dinner.

Once Edward had readied the tender for his shore visit, and he returned to his cabin to hurry Sarah along. He was surprised to hear Sarah decline the trip to shore.

"Sarah, dear, I thought you would join me. I want you to meet…"

Sarah held up her hand to his mouth. "You go and meet him on your own, dear. This is your family. You take this time to get acquainted with him. Then you will introduce me." She kissed him lightly on the cheek, and returned to tidying up the cabin.

Downcast, Edward rowed the boat to the wharf where he would inquire about James Bonnet. He tried to play out in his mind every imaginable conversation he might have with his brother, but nothing sounded quite right.

As he tied up the tender to a bollard on the dock, Edward took in the smells that pervaded the busy wharf. The musky, pungent smell of fish and the muck of tide and human waste mixed with the sweet sugar cane and fruits waiting to be taken aboard another boat. The humid salty air seemed to soothe the blend into one tepid brew of odors so that not one smell overpowered the rest. Edward drew in a long breath as he approached the largest of the gray batten board warehouses that simply labeled, "East Shipping." Not unlike other warehouses he had entered along his journey, this one was filled with activities of selling and dealing and storing. Edward sought out someone in charge, and was directed to a thin black man.

"Excuse me, I am looking for a Mister James Bonnet," Edward said, glancing over his shoulder as he approached the warehouse foreman.

"Mister Bonneet? He is not here, Sir. Perhaps I can help you? My name is Carmen, and I am his agent," said the smiling man in a strong French accent.

"Oh, pleased to meet you, Carmen," Edward shook his hand. "I am Edward Marshall, from the vessel *Anne Marie* there in the harbor." He pointed out the open door that faced the water, as if to offer proof of his business interests. Edward had not anticipated there would be an agent tending to the warehouse business, so he would have to figure out another way to make himself known to James.

"I wonder if Mr. Bonnet will be in later. I was referred to him by a kind woman in St. Philip's Parish."

"If your business is with the warehouse, then I can help you, Mr. Marshall."

"Well, I have an empty cargo hold, and Mrs. Montgomery told me that Mr. Bonnet was the man to see to fill it."

"Mrs. Montgomery? Ah yes, she is a dear lady, and quite astute. If she sent you here for cargo, then *oui*, we can take care of that for you. Come, let us take a look at the manifest, and I can tell you what needs to go where." Carmen pointed ahead to a small office that opened to the harbor. The two men walked in single file through crates stacked three deep and up past Edward's head in such a precarious manner that Edward wondered what would happen if a gust of wind came through the building.

"Please, have a seet, Mr. Marshall," Carmen gestured to a chair on the opposite side of a large mahogany desk stacked high with papers and charts to rival the crates in the warehouse. "Now, what is your destination?" he asked, as he shuffled through the papers first on one side, then on the other side of the desk.

"Well, that depends on the cargo," Edward answered. "We can go just about anywhere, so we are not bound to a destination."

"Ah, you own your ship? Then that changes things a bit. These intra-island trading companies, they are chained to their own pre-set courses, so we have a much harder time accommodating them than we do you 'independents', Mr. Marshall. What is the size of your hold?" Carmen started to fill out a fresh sheet of paper in the ledger, taking down the measurements of the *Anne Marie's* cargo hold and other information. Between answering his questions about potential cargos and destinations, Edward kept a keen eye out for items around the office that might tell him more about his brother.

"Does Mr. Bonnet come to the wharf much, Carmen?" Edward asked as dispassionately as he could.

"Not so much anymore," Carmen said, without looking up from his charts and ledgers. "His health keeps him away. Mostly he stays at his plantation, and I run the warehouse. Do you know him?"

"Only by reputation," Edward tried to sound nonchalant. "I like to meet the men whose cargo I carry, when possible. Mrs. Montgomery spoke so highly of him, you see."

"Yes, he is a good man. I am sure he will be missed. He brought his old plantation back to life after many years of neglect. My own parents once worked for his family, and so I am second generation to his plantation. I come to work here for Mr. Bonneet, and it suits me just fine."

"Your parents? Was it sugar?"

"Yes, back in the day, it was quite a place. I am told there were parties every week. Their mistress, Mr. Bonneet's mother, was a harsh mistress, but she is no longer there. She lives in London with Mr. Bonneet's older brother." Carmen smiled. "I am told that he is as cantankerous as she."

"And Mr. Bonnet. Is he…?"

"No, no. He is a good, fair man. The plantation was in a state of near ruin, and he had to find help to bring it back. My own parents and many others came back to work for him once they realized that he was not like his mother. He had to pay a pretty penny, too, to get the old place back to where it could produce enough to sustain itself again. But it seems to have worked out well enough for the past five years." Carmen looked up, cocked his head to one side, and paused before continuing. "I think he meant to remove himself from his family's side, to come here and relax for his health. I do not think it has done him much good, though."

Edward took in Carmen's words. He thought about how he could get an introduction.

"Would it be appropriate for me to visit him at his plantation? I mean, I wouldn't want to intrude, but I would like to call upon him."

Carmen looked up again from his manifests. "I rather think he would enjoy a visit. He is interested in the colonies, and as you are from there, perhaps you could tell him what he wants to know. I must tell you not to expect a long visit, for he tires easily. We are not sure what we will do when he is… gone, but he assures us that he is providing for us all."

"How many are there?" Edward sat upright in his seat, leaning forward on the desk.

"Only about twenty now. Many have already gained their freedom. As I mentioned, Mr. Bonneet is a fair man, and he sees what is right. He had to sell off some of the land last year, so there was less need for help. I still think he is hoping to regain his health. There are no kin to inherit the plantation or this business. His brother does not want it, and his mother is a little touched, as we say here, so once he is gone…" Carmen shrugged. "But, as I said, he claims we will all be taken care of, and as he is a shrewd businessman, we know he has a plan."

"Well, if it won't be an intrusion, I think I will head to the plantation after we finish our business here. Tell me, what day would you like us to load?" Edward tried hard to look interested in the matter at hand, but in his mind, he was already making his way out of Bridgetown and up the winding road to the Bonnet plantation, just as he had done many a time before as a child.

Edward and Carmen shook hands as they wrapped up their meeting, and Edward politely asked for directions to the plantation.

"Up the main road," Carmen said, pointing up a gentle hill as he escorted Edward to the far warehouse doors that faced Bridgetown. "Keep going up the hill until it winds around to the left. When you think you've missed it, you are just about there. It's about two miles out of town, but if you stay on the main road, you will come to the red pillars at the front gate."

"Red pillars?"

"Yes, there is a story there. It seems some town folk got upset about the senior Mr. Bonneet's activities, and splashed the pillars with red paint as a reminder to others not to follow the same path."

"And what was that…path?" Edward held his breath.

"Well, it is not mine to tell, but the story is well known. I am sure that if you ask Mr. Bonneet, he will tell you himself. Good day to you, Mr. Marshall. We shall look for you in three days for loading." Carmen saluted Edward and turned promptly back to the relative cool of the warehouse, leaving Edward standing at the entrance in the heat of the day.

CHAPTER EIGHTEEN

Edward headed out of town following his memory more so than the directions Carmen offered. He didn't slow his pace until he reached the red pillars. Before he passed through them, he realized this was the first time he'd ever seen them. Hs other ventures to the plantation grounds during his childhood had been around the perimeter, through the canes of sugar, or along the edge of the property through fields of tall grain. Today, he was entering the grounds as a man, yet he felt small as he faced the entrance to his father's home.

Reaching the grand home's columned porch, Edward caught the smell of wisteria on the breeze. He hesitated only a moment before stepping forward and up onto the porch. Taking a breath of the sweet wisteria for courage, he knocked on the massive door. For a fleeting second, he considered retreating. But before he could act, the door opened wide.

"Yassir?" The diminutive woman greeted Edward with a glistening white smile that beamed off her mahogany face.

"I am Edward Marshall, and I've come to call on Mr. Bonnet."

"Yassir, come in here," the woman said, stepping aside to allow Edward to enter. "Wait one minute, and I tell him you here. Do he expect you?"

"No ma'am, I don't believe he does. Carmen at the warehouse said he thought it would be all right for me to call on Mr. Bonnet."

"Carmen? Well, den, I tell the Master you here." She scurried away, her quick short steps under her billowing skirt of pale grey and upheld hands reminding Edward of a rabbit.

Looking around the grand foyer, Edward could see the place's years showing through the wall coverings, faded by the hot sun that streamed in through transoms at the door. A rich staircase wound around to a second level and then to a third which was illuminated by a cupola fashioned with slatted wood wide enough to let the heat escape, but slanted to keep the rain and high winds out. Furnishings were sparse, but what was there was of good quality. It was a pleasant mix of dark wood tables and light wicker chairs and settees whose cushions were draped in pale sheeting that could be aired out or laundered easily.

After a few minutes, James appeared in the hallway behind the stairs, barely visible for the light streaming in through open doors behind him.

"Kesheta tells me Carmen sent you?" James voice strengthened as he drew closer to Edward.

"Yes, Mr. Bonnet? I am Edward Marshall. I do hope you don't mind this intrusion."

"Oh, no, I don't get out much, so visitors are welcome. Please, won't you join me on the back porch? Kesheta was about to fix me something cool to drink. Marshall? I don't think I've heard that name before," James spoke between gasps and coughs. He held his handkerchief over his mouth often as he talked, walking slowly with the assistance of a cane.

"Yes, Edward Marshall. I have come from the colonies, and Carmen suggested you have an interest in them. I have arranged to trade a cargo hold full from your warehouse, so Carmen thought we might like to speak. And truthfully, I prefer to meet the men for whom I trade." Edward walked slowly behind James, taking in his mannerisms, his walk, his looks. James was probably not but six years older than Edward, he guessed. His hair was thick and dark, and his skin was pale from the sickness, Edward surmised. He tried to imagine James as a young boy, searching his memory for anything he might have seen here on the plantation in his own younger days.

"Sit here, Edward," James motioned to a wide wicker chair, while he himself took to a chaise lounge. "Yes, I am very interested in the colonies. I understand they are growing and have much to offer for enterprising souls. I gather that you are an independent?"

"Yes. My wife and I are trading among the islands as we explore this part of the world. It is lovely here. And you are right about the colonies, there are many opportunities. Land is plentiful, and easy to work."

"And where is your wife, now? Is she staying in town?" James' fit of coughing took his breath away.

Edward waited until James regained his composer.

"Blasted consumption." James wiped beads of sweat from his forehead and pocketed his handkerchief.

"No, she has stayed aboard our ship, the *Anne Marie*. We are quite comfortable aboard. She has all the comforts of home."

"Where do you hail from, Edward?" James leaned forward for the cool glass Kesheta offered him. "Tell me about your ship and your plans for trading. I assume Carmen treated you well at the warehouse?"

Edward took his glass from the bamboo tray, and tasted the concoction of what he thought surely contained rum. He was not disappointed. "Carmen was extremely helpful. We will have our load in three days and head southwest. When we come through these waters again, I will be sure to call on your warehouse. Our ship can carry a variety of cargos. I built it myself, so I have equipped it with comfortable accommodations, many from my former home. Many people come through that region by ship, so I learned a good deal about island trade from other people." Edward blushed as he stretched the truth about his association with the likes of Pell. "My wife and I felt it was time to see these places for ourselves, and we have enjoyed the warmth of the waters and the people we've met along our voyage, such as Carmen and yourself. Carmen must be quite capable to run the warehouse by himself."

James looked up at the slats on the porch's ceiling. "Carmen is a good man. His family has been with mine for a very long time. I feel completely safe in leaving that duty to him. I am sure he will continue to manage it in a successful manner, even after I'm dead and gone," James explained, convulsing with coughing. When the fit passed, he sat back in the lounge, and regained his composure.

Edward put his drink down, not knowing if he should stay any longer. "Would you prefer I go?"

"Only if my coughing troubles you. At this point, I am quite used to its interruptions."

"Actually," Edward paused, "I would like to hear the story of the red pillars."

James smiled, and waved his hand as if swatting a fly. "Oh, that. Well, it is quite a story. My father ran this plantation very successfully for many years. When I was two, he did something utterly amazing to everyone here on the island, especially to my mother. He decided at some point to become a pirate, you see. And in the middle of the night, he boarded a ship he claimed was for intra-island trade, surrounded himself with crew found at the local taverns, and left. He gained some notoriety in the next two years, and was known to many as Stede Bonnet, the gentleman pirate.

"My mother didn't find it amusing, but she continued to run this place, and managed to raise my brother and me here without much interference from the town folk until my father was hung in Charleston. Then the world changed, as far as I can remember. The people got mad, and splashed those pillars with red paint, burned some of our smaller outbuildings, and ran off a good number of our help with their threats. My mother moved Philip and me to London--I was about five then.

"The slaves hid out mostly or were roped into working on other plantations here on this island. A few managed to escape, I am told, but I was able to find them and get them back to work a few years ago when I returned."

"And what of your mother and your brother?"

"They still reside in London, much enamored with the lifestyle they've cultivated there. I cared nothing for their fancy parties. My mother became a bit of a celebrity herself, you see, what with being the wife of a pirate and all, so she and Philip have had a good ride on that story as well."

"Did you have any other siblings?" Edward hedged.

"Some years ago when I returned to the island, some of the older folks inquired if I was the 'other' child. At the time, I surmised that they were thinking I was Philip, but I later learned that my father was, well, he was busy elsewhere when I was an infant." He sipped his drink.

"You don't seem upset by this story."

"As children, we had no idea what our father was, or even how he died. We were very sheltered. In London, there was really far too much for us to do to ponder such things. We went to fine schools, we traveled, and we ate well. My father's reputation seemed more of a calling card to the best of parties and families rather than a detriment. I really just never gave it any thought then. It was only after I moved back here that I heard there might have been another child, and I began to wonder what it must have been like for a bastard child of my father, growing up knowing who he was."

"It was terrible." Edward looked down at his hands. He hadn't meant to say it.

"I beg your pardon, Edward?" James leaned forward slightly, putting his drink down on the table beside him.

"I said that it was terrible. I…I don't know how to tell you this, other than to come right out and say it: *I am the pirate's bastard.*"

James sat back, his face emotionless. Edward's words washed over him like a gentle rain. Slowly, a smile formed on his thin lips.

"So you *do* exist." His words hung like a veil, draping softly over the two of them as they faced each other on the veranda. "I wondered what you were like. Where did you get the red hair?" James pointed a boney finger at Edward's tussle of red.

Edward brushed his hand through his thick hair and smiled. "My mother, I am told." Relieved, he relaxed in his chair. "I've wondered about you ever since I learned I had siblings."

"And when was that?"

"Not long ago, just before our voyage began," Edward explained.

"Did you come in search of me?"

"I came in search of answers. I did not know you were still here, and only learned about your presence from Mrs. Montgomery. I was born in the house where she stays, and wanted to see it. She was a gracious hostess, and directed me to your warehouse."

For several hours, Edward unraveled his story for James, and the two brothers answered each other's questions. It was not until the light from the setting sun colored the pale walls of the house tangerine that Edward realized the time.

"I must be getting back to the ship. I am sure my wife is wondering what's become of me." He stood to leave.

James struggled to get up, and slowly escorted Edward to the door. "I hope you will bring her tomorrow. I would like to meet her, and I suspect she is as curious about me as you were. It is a rare thing that long-lost family members meet, and I should like to get to know mine as much as I can before... before you set sail. How long will you be in the islands?"

"For a few weeks," Edward was slow to answer. He had not thought about what came after this voyage. "If you are up for it, perhaps you would like to join us aboard the ship for dinner one evening. Sarah is a fine cook."

"Perhaps. Sometimes traveling even to the wharf is difficult for me," James said, as he opened the door for Edward. "Come back around again. I would like to have more time with you, 'Brother,' before you leave Barbados. It seems we have much to talk about, and I am not keen on losing you after only knowing you for so short a time."

Edward agreed to return, and started the walk to the main road as the sky turned deep orange streaked with pink. Tonight would be a calm night, he thought. Calm, indeed.

CHAPTER NINETEEN

The walk back was filled with the sounds of an island settling in for the evening. Edward pondered all that he had learned, and where it would take him next. He tried to calculate the value of staying in Barbados to be with his brother or going back to the colonies so that he and Sarah could make amends with her family, if she wanted to. He was torn, realizing that once again his past could possibly challenge his future. James' health was failing, that was clear; but at least for a time, Edward could enjoy James, and perhaps the two brothers' reconciliation would be sufficient to shoo away the past's haunting. He would talk with Sarah, and together they could make plans.

Edward rowed steadily through the calm waters of the harbor toward the ship. Few lanterns were lit, but he made his way to the rope ladder amidships and climbed aboard.

"Sarah?" He called, as he headed for their aft cabin. There was no response. He moved forward to the galley, but the stove was cold, the table untouched.

Edward wondered if perhaps Sarah and his crew rowed to town for an evening meal, but as he made his way back through the companionway, he noticed a shiny spot of dark liquid on the steps, then another, and another. He followed the trail to the starboard side and saw the lines to the second launch were slashed. The dinghy was gone!

Edward scrambled across the deck and down the ladder to his launch and rowed furiously to the harbor's main wharf. Where was Sarah? Where was his crew? He had no idea where to look first at this time of the evening as he ran from the town's docks and asked the first person he saw if there was a doctor in town, and then ran up the hill to a tidy red-tiled white cottage that gleamed in a wash of the night's pale moonlight. Slowing only long enough to catch his breath, Edward caught sight of Jolly slumped on the steps.

"Jolly!" Edward's pitch was frantically high. "What happened?" He leapt up the steps and was about to enter the building when Jolly caught his leg like a Venus Fly Trap snaps its prey.

"We didn't know what else to do...she just kept screaming," Jolly met Edward's stare. Then, just as quickly as he grabbed it, Jolly released Edward's leg, as if granting him permission to enter the candle-lit room.

A black woman with a pancake-shaped face as round as her waist came to the door, a quietness surrounding her. "Are you kin?" Her hushed tones suggested the gravity of the situation.

As Edward nodded, she pulled his arm gently into a second, smaller and darker room filled with strange, almost volatile smells that brought a hint of tears to Edward's eyes. And when his teary eyes adjusted to the dim room, he saw Sarah on a small wooden-framed cot with a sheet pulled up to her chin. She was shivering despite the humid temperature.

Within two steps Edward was at her side and kneeling, gently picking up her hand in his.

"Sarah, my darling, I am here," he whispered as he stroked her forehead.

"She can't hear you, Mista. She been through a lot today," the woman stood just behind Edward, then tapped him on the shoulder, motioning for him to follow. Reluctantly, Edward obeyed. "They brought her to me, I am Miss Catrine, de midwife, Mista," she said as she pulled a curtain that separated the two rooms. "Is you her man?"

"Yes." The word "midwife" struck home, and he started to head back into the room where his wife lay. "I didn't know she was…is she going to…?"

"She is very weak, Mista. She had a bad time, I tell you. But when she wake up, we know more. I call for de doctor, he will know what to do."

"Edward, we are sorry. We didn't know what else to do, so we found this place," Clarence talked from just outside the door, looking afraid to cross the threshold. "We didn't have time to find a doctor, Edward. Miss Sarah was bleeding and screaming, and just getting her off the ship was painful to her."

Edward straightened his shoulders and entered the small dark room again to sit with Sarah. Slumping on the floor beside her, he whispered her name.

"Sarah, you must get strong again. We have so much to discuss, so much to do together." He placed her small, cold hand in his, and stroked the back of it gently. "Your hands are cold, dear. No matter, I will see if there is another blanket about. I want to tell you of my visit with James. He is a kind man, not anything like our father from what I could gather today. He wants to meet you, so when you are able to have a visitor …." Edward's throat grew dry, and his eyes brimmed with tears. Sarah gave no recognition of his presence. "Sarah? Can you hear me? Please, Sarah, wake up."

But there was no response.

Miss Catrine entered undetected, and took Sarah's hand from Edward. After a brief moment, she placed it under the sheet, and then began to raise the sheet over Sarah's ashen face.

"No!" yelled Edward and he jumped up to pull the sheet back, but Miss Catrine held him firmly at bay.

"You got no right to disturb her now, Mista. She go to a betta' place, where de ain't no pain." Her voice was even, yet quiet. She started to pray over Sarah, with one heavy arm still holding Edward away from Sarah's lifeless figure on the cot.

Edward ran from the cottage, not heeding Jolly or Clarence as they ran after calling his name. When he stopped running, he realized he was at the red pillars.

The midwife's words rang in his ears over and over. "You got no right … a betta' place …" Her words could apply to him here in Barbados as well. He really had no right to be there. He too would have to find his "betta' place". He held himself up against a red pillar, then slowly walked back to the cottage.

Clarence and Jolly were waiting for him on the front porch. In the faint light of moon and stars, he entered the cottage, and reemerged carrying Sarah. The three moved quietly down the hill and through the sandy streets to the town dock, and then they carefully lowered Sarah's body into one of the launches. Edward mechanically untied the small craft from the wharf, and rowed out to the ship. Clarence and Jolly followed in the other launch, and assisted Edward in boarding with Sarah in his arms. Without a word, Clarence and Jolly weighed anchor, and set their course. Edward wrapped Sarah in his favorite quilts and lay her in the aft cabin. Then he closed the door.

The passage was swift. When they reached the southerly tip of the lonely island, Edward moved forward and dropped the anchor. In the dark of night, the three men picked their way over the shoals in a single launch that towed a second. A lantern lit the dune, then a gnarled oak tree.

Before the morning sun shimmered its rays on the beach, Edward and his small crew finished their task. Quietly, slowly, they rowed back to the ship.

As the new day's sun stretched its rays toward the gnarled tree like a lover's arms longing for one last embrace, a new voyage would begin where another one ended. Smith Island would forever hold the secret treasures of a father and a son, unitewd by death after all.

THE END

LEAVING LUKENS

By Laura S. Wharton

Print ISBN: 978-0-9837148-0-4

eBook ISBN: 978-0-9837148-1-1

Publisher: Broad Creek Press, 2011

Summary: As friends move from the safe enclave of Lukens that always has been her home, Ella Hutchins struggles with the decision to leave the disappearing coastal town near Oriental. Her choice might be made for her when World War II edges closer to the North Carolina village, but not before a visiting sailor named Griff teaches her how to see anew treasures of life both above and below the ocean's surface. Is Griff really what he appears to be? *Leaving Lukens* is a fast-paced historical adventure that will leave readers spell-bound until the surprising end!

Nominated for SIBA (Southeastern Independent Booksellers Association) Fiction Award, The Janet Heidinger Kafka Prize for Fiction by an American Woman and BRAG Medallion honoree for 2013.

Published Reviews of Leaving Lukens

Chosen as Reviewer's Choice by Midwest Book Reviews

Fine Work of Historical Fiction

The allure of life can quickly be soured by the truth. Leaving Lukens is a novel set around the eve of World War II, and follows Ella Marie Hutchens as she lives her life in a small North Carolinian fishing village and meets Griff. But as time marches on, she quickly finds Griff has many secrets and few of them are good. Leaving Lukens is a fine work of historical fiction and romance, highly recommended.

~ Midwest Book Reviews

Bittersweet Story

Wharton is excellent at describing her characters and in creating a historical atmosphere. She has clearly researched the time period, the music, the details of the Navy and other military affairs during World War II, and the history of Lukens itself. She writes with a grace and smoothness, and despite her book having a Nazi subplot, she does not rely on sensationalism or extreme plot twists to gain her readers' attention. She creates nostalgia and wistfulness in her writing without falling into sentimentality, and in the end, the reader fully understands all the reasons why Ella, the main character, does not want to leave Lukens, along with the reasons she finds for wanting to start over. Far more than a story about the war, Leaving Lukens is about finding happiness, and finding that home is in the heart and not a physical place.

~ Tyler R. Tichelaar, Ph.D., author of the award-winning *Narrow Lives*

Steamy, Spell-Binding Story

Leaving Lukens is part fast-paced adventure, part historical fiction, and part steamy summer romance that will leave the reader spell-bound until the surprising end! A fine read!

> ~ Mary Flinn, author of *The One, Second Time's a Charm*, and *Three Gifts*

Ending Blew Me Away

I have read Ms. Wharton's first book, The Pirate's Bastard. I did enjoy it a lot. Yet, as I began to read this book, I found she was not just a onetime author. In fact I enjoyed this book even more than the first. I loved the characters in this book and the way, Ms. Wharton has created them. The flow of the story is excellent and I did not find even one page or paragraph that was boring. The book starts on May 2000 at a reunion and then goes back to WWII. There we find adventure, love and intrigue. The ending blew me away. I had to read it twice and then it hit me. (It was a slap me silly moment for me.) Just one sentence told me what I longed to hear. I did not want this story to end. Nor do I think you will either, and that is why I am giving this book a five star rating.

> ~Sandra Heptinstall, Reviewer

A novel about growing and moving on with your life

Once I started reading this book I really got involved with it. Ella was so easy to get connected with. The novel is about growing up and moving on with one's life. There are a few intense moments in the book dealing with the war, but mainly the story revolves around the life of Ella and Griff. I enjoyed the atmosphere of the novel, the location and the historical aspect. If you are looking for a historical novel that will keep you entertained from beginning to end, and then grab a copy of Leaving Lukens. This is the first book that I have read by this author but I found it very enlightening and I feel you will, too.

~Miss Lynn, Book Reviewer

A Good Read

The book moved at a good pace and the historical details seemed well-researched. It was a good read and the characters were believable; I enjoyed the story. I could see this as a made-for-TV movie. I like this author's books.

~North Carolina Reader

Exciting New Adventure

In June of 1942, Lukens is a small town on the North Carolina coast, and it's getting smaller. Residents left first in trickles, but now they're crossing the Neuse in a torrent to places like Oriental, with its modern conveniences and thriving community. Ella Marie Hutchins, seventeen, is dead set against leaving. Everything she loves is in Lukens: her house, her Grandmother, and her handsome boyfriend, soon-to-be naval officer Jarrett Migette. When Jarrett announces he's leaving earlier than planned, and her mother decides that they're moving, Ella is distraught. Leaving Lukens might be the safest idea, however, as the war is closer than anyone thinks. Walking alone near the tideline one evening, Ella is threatened by a vicious Nazi scout, and barely escapes unscathed. Luckily, she's assisted by a young stranger named Griff, who just happens to be passing by. Griff's story makes sense—he's a recreational sailor and treasure-hunter, visiting his uncle in Lukens on his prize sailboat Susanna. Soon he and Ella are fast friends, and as they spend more time together sailing, biking, and picnicking throughout the long, hot, Lukens summer, they begin to feel more for one another. But Griff is more than he seems, and the secret mission he is bound to fulfill will push Ella into danger greater than she's ever faced before.

Filled with sailing lore, secrecy, Nazis, and romance, Leaving Lukens is an exciting new adventure from the author of The Pirate's Bastard. Check this title's availability in the UNC-Chapel Hill Library catalog.

~Read North Carolina Novels

Packed with Adventure and Mystery

Leaving Lukens opens in the year 2000 with Ella Marie Hutchins returning to her childhood home for a reunion of the families of Lukens. Ella was only 17 years old in 1942, when World War II hit her small coastal town hard, and residents quickly moved away to larger areas with better jobs. As she looks back over that year, she recalls the hardship of leaving home, and the young man that changed her perspective on the future. Interspersed throughout this historical romance are vignettes of life during wartime that bring the fear of the Nazis to the forefront. I was especially impressed with Ms. Wharton's grasp of the historical during this time period, especially regarding the innocence and embedded fear of the War. Much research had to have been done regarding the area and its people, and it is evident in the content of the story. While a topic such as the Nazis could take over a story, the characters in Leaving Lukens are what truly shine. Ella is a young girl conflicted with the changes in her life, but soon learns to come to terms with the future. Griff, meanwhile, is a mysterious force that beckons to Ella, changing her future, forever.

Leaving Lukens reads so smoothly you can devour it in no time. It is engrossing in its theme, and in its lyrical style. Part historic fiction, part romance, packed with adventure and mystery, it holds your attention throughout. The ending was very climactic, and surprising. I truly hated to see it end, but enjoyed every minute spent in its pages.

~Literary R&R

Another Five-Star Novel by Laura S. Wharton

Deception, deceit, loyalty, friendship and so much more are part of this outstanding and intricate plot. As Ella becomes more involved in Griff's world we see a marked change in her. Through meeting his friends, helping him on his boat, diving, treasure hunting and much more, Ella grows up right before the reader's eyes and her perspective changes as the enemy is not only those called Nazi, but others hiding in plain sight. This is a great historical novel and I would love to learn more about Lukens before the War. From the author of The Pirate's Bastard comes another Five Star Novel--or in this case, FIVE SPANISH TREASURED GOLD COINS.

~Fran Lewis, *New Year* Reviewer

AVAILABLE IN PAPERBACK OR E-BOOKS
WHEREVER FINE BOOKS ARE SOLD.

Children's Books by Laura S. Wharton:

Mystery at the Lake House #1: Monsters Below

Mystery at the Phoenix Festival

CPSIA information can be obtained at www.ICGtesting.com
Printed in the USA
LVOW13s1849010913

350506LV00001B/1/P